"Hot, hot, HOT!"

—Mystique Book Reviews

BEAUTY, EXCESS, *FREEDOM*

Of all the idiot assignments Kiley Trevor has suffered as a private investigator, this one takes the cake. Flying to Mistral Cay sounded grand until she learned Julian St. John's private island was basically a sex retreat for rich, bored women, and the mysterious Julian is King of the Man-Whores. Kiley's assignment? Find the gigolo with a birthmark on his...privates.

From the minute he saw her, Julian St. John knew "Ms. Trevor" was different—and not just from her proffered identity. Uncovering her lies would help protect his secrets and tortured past. Uncovering the rest of her would set him free.

"An unforgettable story that leaves a mark long after it is over."

—Coffeetime Romance Reviews

WILD ISLAND WINDS

Charlotte Boyett-Compo

www.BOROUGHSPUBLISHINGGROUP.com

WILD ISLAND WINDS
Copyright © 2015 Charlotte Boyett-Compo

ISBN 978-1-942886-83-9

To Stormy Storms. You need a Julian in your life, babe! Don't we all?

CONTENTS

WILD ISLAND WINDS

Chapter One

"The birthmark is on the guy's scrotum," Kiley Trevor reminded her flying companion.

"Then you'll have to lift up his cock to look for it. What better way to get a good look at that pecker."

Kiley sighed heavily. "I was hoping you'd do the looking and I could do the photographing," she said.

"Nope," Dr. Olivia Carstairs replied with a shake of her elegant head. "I'll be otherwise engaged while we're there. The extent of my involvement in this case of yours is to introduce you to the proprietor of Mistral Cay, Julian St. John, and to give you a bit of medical knowledge so you'll appear legitimate."

Of all the bullshit assignments Kiley Trevor had suffered while working as an investigator for Heartland Investigative Services, this one took the cake. While the cause was worthy—finding the adult son of a woman forced to give up him up when he was two years old—the only clue to his identity was a distinctive birthmark on the man's scrotum. And, of course, this couldn't be easy. The guy worked at an exclusive high-class resort that catered to wealthy bored women. Read: man-whore. Fabu-fuckin-lous.

Helen, their first-class flight attendant, came to take their drink orders, saving Kiley from responding to Dr. Carstairs's refusal to help find the man they were going to Mistral Cay to find.

"I'll have a Bloody Maria," Kiley said. "Tequila, not vodka. Lots of lime." *God knows I need it. If I wasn't two delinquent bills away from bankruptcy, I'd tell those shithead bosses of mine where to stuff it.*

"Sounds good to me," Dr. Carstairs agreed. "Never had a Bloody Mary that way before. Bloody Maria, you said?"

"That's what they call it in Texas," Kiley replied.

"Umm. Is that where you're from?"

"Yes, ma'am. San Antonio."

"I was born and raised in London," Dr. Carstairs said. "About as western as I've ever been is riding some of the young studs at the resort. Now that will make you sit up straight in the saddle and shout tally-ho." She nudged Kiley's shoulder with her own.

Kiley was saved again from responding when Helen brought their drinks.

"Now, this I like," Dr. Carstairs pronounced and took a healthy swig. Without asking, she thrust her skewer of olives into Kiley's glass but kept the rib of celery that also garnished the drink. "You need to lighten up, dearie," Dr. Carstairs commented. "Bring us another one, would you, Helen?"

Kiley hadn't been aware of the flight attendant passing her seat. She glanced up and nodded at Helen's raised eyebrow.

"And bring us some more celery," Dr. Carstairs ordered.

Fifteen minutes later, with two potent Bloody Marias under her belt, Kiley's nerves settled and her tongue loosened.

"The thought of photographing strange men's penises is weird."

"You'll get over it," Dr. Carstairs laughed. "It's not like you're doing it to arouse them."

"Lord, I hope that doesn't happen," Kiley moaned.

"Well, the possibility is very good that it will, but if you should be required to interview with Julian, be sure to tell him you don't wish to participate in the sexual activities offered at the resort. Tell him you're there strictly as my assistant, doing research for me."

"What's he like?"

"Julian?" Dr. Carstairs asked. She took the last bite of her celery before answering then shifted in her seat so she could look at Kiley. "You know those panthers you see pacing their cages in the zoo?"

"Panthers?" Kiley echoed.

"Their sleek black coats glisten in the sun. Their powerful muscles ripple beneath that taut skin," Dr. Carstairs described. "You know they are dangerous, that they could tear you apart with those ferocious teeth and curved claws, but you are mesmerized by all that sheer male beauty. Those golden eyes hold you spellbound and you feel small and insignificant beside them."

"I'm more fond of Maine Coon kitty cats myself," Kiley confessed.

Dr. Carstairs waved her hand in dismissal. "Give me a man like Julian St. John any day. There is power and authority, and such potent sexuality. He is scrumptious."

"And I bet he charges more if he's the one to service you," Kiley sniffed.

"Oh, he never fraternizes with his clients," Dr. Carstairs said. "There is one woman who comes to the Cay twice a year or so and stays in his personal apartments but I don't think she's his woman; rather, she's a good friend." She thought for a moment. "He's quite private."

"Perhaps he's gay."

The urologist laughed. "I wouldn't consider that for even a minute."

"You never know. He owns the resort?" Kiley asked for clarification.

"Owns and runs it with an iron hand." Dr. Carstairs leaned closer and lowered her voice though no one was within earshot of them. "An iron hand I've love to have caressing me."

"In other words his word is law there."

Dr. Carstairs nodded. "He owns the entire island, so in essence he's also the governing body of Mistral Cay."

"Must be a very rich man."

"I would think so. I heard somewhere that he comes from old money, grew up in Europe and was educated at the finest schools, but that he doesn't use his real name. Too bad because I'd love to know who the family is." Dr. Carstairs sighed heavily. "He has all the prerequisites for a superb husband if he was inclined to marry, which I'm told he is not." She snorted. "Given my own experience with the bonds of matrimony, I don't think that's such a bad thing."

"I take it he's the kind of man you find attractive."

"Well it's the mystery surrounding him, don't you know," the older woman replied. "He keeps to himself, lives alone except for his male housekeeper Christian, and Henri Bouvier, his administrative assistant. I've never seen him in anything but unrelieved black—silk shirts, leather britches, form-fitting pullovers, black T-shirts and black jeans. That particular choice of clothing color may be intentional for it underscores and accentuates the mysteriousness, you see." She put up one finger. "The only hint of color is the gold hoop in his left ear."

"Like I said, he's probably gay."

Dr. Carstairs clucked her tongue. "Don't believe it for a minute."

Kiley yawned. The liquor had gone to her head and she was relaxed enough to fall off.

"Why don't you take a little snoozer?" Dr. Carstairs suggested. "I could do with a few winks myself."

"I didn't get much sleep last night," Kiley confessed.

"Then close those pretty little eyes and slip into dreamland." The urologist put a finger to the side of her nose. "Dream of young hunky men with extra-long tallywhackers to slide into your sugar and give you a rip-roaring orgasm."

Despite the scarlet stain she felt overtake her cheeks, Kiley laughed. She had liked the English doctor from the moment she had met her over two years earlier as a client, but the woman had a tendency to embarrass Kiley with her salty mannerisms.

"I may just do that," Kiley replied.

Sleep didn't take long to find Kiley with the drone of the plane's engine, the comfort of the extra-wide leather seat and the soft pillow Helen provided. Aided by the potency of the tequila, the young woman slipped easily into the waiting arms of Morpheus.

She was jostled awake by a bit of turbulence. She sat up straighter in her seat and looked at her companion. Dr. Carstairs was snoring lightly, a thin stream of drool oozing from the corner of her slack mouth. Another jolt of turbulence made Kiley grip the arms of her seat.

"Ladies and gentlemen," the announcement came over the address system. "We are experiencing some mild turbulence at this time. Please fasten your seatbelts and return your tray tables to the upright position. We will be climbing to forty thousand to get above the bad weather and do not anticipate any further inconvenience. We will keep you informed."

"I don't suppose they'll be serving drinks anytime soon," Dr. Carstairs complained as she wiped at the spittle on her chin.

"I imagine not," Kiley agreed.

"Did you get some shut-eye?"

"Yes."

"Me," Dr. Carstairs began, "I dreamt I was lying on the beach at Mistral Cay with Julian's head in my lap." She stretched, listing her hands over her head. "We were naked as the day we were born."

Kiley smiled. "You've got a thing for the resort owner, don't you?"

"I'd give that man anything he wanted," the urologist replied. She laid her head back against the seat as the plane began its slow ascent to the higher elevation. "I once offered to take him to Hong Kong with me but he declined. It seems he never leaves the Cay."

"Never?" Kiley asked, one brow cocked in surprise.

"That's what he said."

"I wonder why."

"I've asked him many times and he always comes up with the most entertaining reasons," Dr. Carstairs said with a grin.

"Such as?"

"Oh, once it was because he had an incurable disease and if he left the curative waters of the Cay, he'd succumb to the illness and die a horrible, lingering death. A variation on that theme was if he left the Cay, he'd age like the portrait of Dorian Gray, turn into dust and blow away. Another time he hinted that he was an international fugitive hiding out from both the C.I.A. and K.G.B." She laughed. "And then there was the explanation that he was actually a vampire and couldn't cross running water."

"An imaginative man," Kiley said.

"Imaginative, alluring, seductive. You think of any adjective that describes a dream man and you've got Julian St. John."

"I can't wait to meet this paragon of male superiority," Kiley mumbled.

"Just be careful around him," Dr. Carstairs warned. "He is intuitive. If he suspects you are there for any other purpose than what we've rehearsed, he could send you packing."

Kiley let out a long sigh. "Well, all I want to do is find the man I'm—"

"The cock," Dr. Carstairs giggled, "you're looking for."

"The birthmark," Kiley corrected.

"Your boss, Greg Strickland, didn't say why you're looking for this bloke," the urologist said. "Is he in trouble of some kind?"

"Why would you think so?"

"It just seems an odd way of trying to locate a man, getting a peeper at his pecker, I mean. Why can't you just ask if John Doe or Bill Smith or whatever his name is works at the resort?"

"I shouldn't be discussing this with you, but since Greg has involved you, I guess you have a right to a few facts. For one thing, we don't know the name the young man is using," Kiley replied. "And we don't know what he looks like. It's his mother who is looking for him and she hasn't seen him since he was two years old."

"Why ever not?"

"He was taken away from her and given up for adoption."

Dr. Carstairs nodded. "A bad mother, was she?"

"From all accounts, she was a wonderful mother, but she committed a crime and was sent to prison."

"Ah," the urologist drawled. "I begin to see the picture. What crime did she commit?"

"I'm not at liberty to answer that. Let's just say it was a felony that required a rather lengthy stay in federal prison."

"And when she was released, she began searching for her son?"

"According to Mr. Strickland's partner, Ross Bennis, she'd been trying to find him from the very start, but the state wouldn't give her any information. When she got out, she contacted several private investigation firms and that's how Heartland became involved."

"Not an inexpensive process," Dr. Carstairs commented. "Where did she come up with the money to do this?"

"I don't know, ma'am, and couldn't tell you if I did."

The urologist clucked her tongue impatiently. "If she doesn't know his adopted name, doesn't know what he looks like, how will she—?"

"She can identify him by the birthmark on his scrotum," Kiley reminded her.

"All right, I understand that, but why does she believe he is at Julian's resort?"

Kiley rubbed her forehead. "Dr. Carstairs, the lady moves in circles not unlike your own and she overheard two women at a party talking about male escorts. She found the conversation distasteful and was walking away when one happened to mention the strange birthmark she had seen on her sexual partner's scrotum."

"That had to be a helluva shock," Dr. Carstairs chuckled. "I can't begin to imagine how I would feel hearing my son had become a male escort."

"I'm sure our client was both shocked and hopeful that she'd found her missing son. She questioned the women and found out the man in question had once worked in New Orleans but was now thought to be at the Cay, though neither woman had been invited to visit the resort so they weren't sure if he was there or not. She learned all she could about Mistral Cay then contacted the P.I.

agencies with whom she was working. The only one who would agree to send someone to the resort was Heartland."

"Ross Bennis's greed to the forefront," Dr. Carstairs quipped.

"That's how Greg sees it, yes."

"So what happens when you find the young man? Do you tell him his mother is looking for him?"

"That was considered to be a risky way of handling it. He might not even know he was adopted or he might think his mother is deceased. There was also the concern that he wouldn't want to meet her. He might be too ashamed or he just might be a cad who couldn't care less. It was decided that I was to offer him a considerable incentive to come to the U.S. in the form of an employment opportunity."

"Cost being of no importance I take it."

"Something like that."

"Well, either she embezzled a large amount of money that has been drawing interest in a secret Swiss bank account or she married Mr. Moneybags or has something on Mr. Moneybags if she can afford sending the two of us to the resort," Dr. Carstairs observed.

"Let's just say she can afford it and leave it at that."

Dr. Carstairs tapped the side of her finger against her lip. "Now I wonder which society maven I know is the driving force behind this little scenario. I wager I've met this woman."

"She's a mother searching for her child, Dr. Carstairs. She should have our sympathy rather than conjecture, don't you think?"

As the journey drew out, Kiley stared out the window and speculated what it would feel like to discover your child had fallen into a profession upon which most people would look down. Her own parents thought her chosen work as a private investigator was unseemly as well as sordid. Would they have disowned her if she had fallen into the squalid world of prostitution?

"Damned right they would have," Kiley murmured.

She had to admire Mrs. Lynden for wanting to find her son no matter what he did for money. She only wondered if finding him would be in the woman's best interests.

Chapter Two

Fay Lynden lay beside her sleeping husband and thanked the gods she had a man like Bradford Lynden.

Now all she needed was her son to make life complete once more.

A single hitch of breath escaped her mouth as she thought of the little boy who had been torn from her arms that day over thirty years ago. Her wild cries, her struggles, had not moved the government officials who had come to take her child away. Her last sight of the son she had named Patrick was his little face—scrunched up in a horrific howl—as the social worker buckled him in the car seat. She would never forget his little outstretched arms, his tiny fists beating against the glass as he was driven out of her life.

Prison had been only a minor circle of hell for Fay O'Reilly. Her true punishment had been the absence of her little boy and the torture of not knowing if he was alive or dead, of wondering if he was being cared for and loved or if he was being abused. The most terrible day of her life had been the day she learned her precious child had been adopted by some nameless family. Patrick would never know her as the woman who had given him birth and who loved him still more than life itself.

"It's the best thing for him," the social worker sniffed, "and I'm sure you want the best for the boy."

As the years passed, her son's memory remained bright and clear in Fay's mind and the determination to find him once she had served her time never wavered. She wrote him every day even though she knew her letters would never be forwarded to the family who had adopted him. In those letters she poured out her soul, explained how and why she had wound up in the nightmarish prison that kept her from him; she begged his forgiveness for what she had been forced to do.

On the day she was finally released from her hellish incarceration, she had stood outside the prison gates in the pouring rain, her face to the heavens, tears mingling with the raindrops and vowed that no matter what it took, or how long, she would find her son, now a grown man.

Trudging down the interstate, cheap suitcase containing all her worldly possessions clutched in her cold hand, she had passed the sign warning motorists not to pick up hitchhikers. Resolved to walk all the way to the next town, she had been surprised when the expensive white Lincoln Town Car's brake lights came on and it pulled off the slab just ahead of her. Cautiously approaching the idling car, she had flinched as the front passenger door swung open when she drew near.

He was leaning down in the seat so he could see her beneath the barrier of the door opening. "Hop in," he said. "You'll catch your death of cold out there."

While her people gauge had been skewed by prison life, she recognized something warm and non-threatening in his open face. He was smiling at her in a way no man had in a long, long time.

"Can't you read, Mister?" she had asked, nudging her chin toward the sign warning motorists not to pick up hitchhikers.

"Yes, I can," he replied. "And I can do math, too. Been able to since I was knee high to a possum's belly."

Watching his infectious grin widen, she had figured he'd be a means to an end and would help her get to a place where she could start looking for Patrick. She accepted the stranger's offer, and, as the years would prove, she never once regretted her decision.

"Where you headed?" he inquired as he pulled the car onto the interstate.

"You can drop me wherever is convenient for you. I got nowhere to go and no time to get there."

"Done your time and don't have to worry about a parole officer, huh?" he asked.

Fay O'Reilly had stared at the middle-aged man behind the wheel. "How'd you know I—"

"The Correctional Institute for Women is back there," the man interrupted, jerking his thumb over his shoulder. "I imagine that's where you were."

"Do you make it a habit to pick up ex-cons?" she snapped.

"Only ones who look like cute little wet puppies," he responded, glancing over at her. "You give new meaning to having a bad hair day, little lady."

Fay turned her attention to the front of the car, staring out the windshield at the rain lashing against the glass. Eastward, lightning flared in the sky. As grateful as she was to be inside the warm car, she was suspicious of her companion.

"My name is Bradford Lynden," the driver said. "I live in Altoona but I'm on my way to Davenport for a meeting."

"Fay O'Reilly," she supplied. "Davenport sounds good."

Her companion was quiet for a moment then cleared his throat. Out of the corner of her eye, she saw him gripping the steering wheel so tightly his knuckles had bled of color.

"Look here," he said, clearing his throat before he continued. "If you need some money to help you—"

"That's what I figured," Fay hissed. "Just pull over and let me out right now."

She saw his head swivel toward her. "Ma'am, I think you misunderstood me," he said quickly.

"Stop the damned car and let me out," she shouted.

Lynden put on his turn signal and slid cautiously onto the breakdown lane. He glanced in the rearview mirror as he braked then put on his emergency blinkers. Even before the car stopped moving, Fay was fumbling at the door handle.

"Now, wait just a minute," Lynden growled, reaching for Fay's arm. Her response to his touch stunned them both—the crack of her palm meeting his face echoed through the car.

The fiery red handprint on his left cheek could be seen clearly even in the dismal light cast from the storm. As rivulets of water cascaded down the windshield, thunder rumbled overhead and lightning flared around them, the wind buffeted the idling car, rocking it as traffic skirled by on the superhighway. It seemed the bottom had fallen out of the sky for the volume of the rain suddenly increased.

"You know, I believe we're on the edge of a wall cloud," Lynden said in an uneasy voice.

Fay blinked. "A tornado?"

"Just listen," he said.

Off in the distance, there was a low droning sound that might well be coming from the train tracks running parallel to the interstate. Driver and passenger looked at one another.

"We're not that far from an overpass," Lynden said. "I believe we'd better make for it."

Nodding her acceptance, Fay kept her fingers wrapped around the door handle as her companion eased the town car back onto the highway. She realized he hadn't turned off the emergency blinkers and that his face was strained in the glow from the dashboard lights.

"I don't like bad weather," Fay commented.

"It's all right as long as you're inside a sturdy building," Lynden stated, "but I don't care for it at all when I'm out driving in it."

The rhythmic slap of the windshield wipers was so fast their movement was giving Fay a queasy feeling as she tried to peer out the glass. There was limited visibility and the flare of lightning pulses further obscured the highway.

"The overpass should be just up ahead. Let's hope nobody else is parked under it," Lynden said.

The droning sound was getting louder, the rumble of a runaway train coming at them from the south side of the interstate.

"Hurry," Fay said.

Lynden hunched over the steering wheel and reached up to wipe away the condensation that was forming on the windshield. He glanced at his passenger when she slid toward him and used the sleeve of her blouse to help clear the fogged area.

Fay could feel the car shuddering beneath her rump. The wind was shrieking so loudly she couldn't hear his words but she realized he was pointing toward a dark shape just up ahead. She nodded.

One moment they were rolling to a stop beneath the overpass, the next Bradford Lynden was shoving her out the passenger door, scurrying after her then pulling her with him up the concrete incline and under the soaring rafters.

Wind and flying debris were pummeling them, stinging their flesh and blinding them as they climbed as high as the concrete slope would allow. A deafening roar drowned out any other sound as Lynden pulled her head against his chest, arched his upper body over hers and wrapped his legs around her hips. Wedged tightly into the triangular section of concrete between the bridge overhead and the incline, she held onto his waist with all her might while he wrapped his arms around the steel girder above them.

For what seemed like an eternity, the sound of the tornado—the shrill flute of its movement—traveled the length of the overpass. The girders hummed, the concrete sang and the accompanying music of flying debris chimed in harmony with the plaintive voice of the fierce, deadly wind. Fay kept her eyes tightly closed, her arms squeezing Bradford Lynden, her cheek pressed to his chest where she could hear the wild beat of his heart as he strained to keep them attached to the girder.

She felt Bradford's legs trembling as he anchored her to him while the wind pulled at him and strained his arms, trying to suck the two of them away from their hiding place. Something had struck the back of his head and she could feel the warmth of his blood oozing down his neck trickling onto her clasped hands. By the time the howl of the wind had died down to a fading rumble to the north of them, he was unconscious, the loss of blood having taken its toll, but his legs were locked around Fay O'Reilly's hips, keeping her safe.

As he had kept her safe for four years now, she thought as she wedged herself against his sleeping body. Even in sleep, he reached out to put an arm around her, anchoring her securely to him.

"We'll find your boy, darlin'," Bradford had promised and over the years had done everything he could to keep that vow.

Rich beyond Fay's wildest dreams, powerful as any state politician could ever be, her transplanted Alabama boy had provided her with wealth and position, a stunning home and happiness that knew no boundaries.

If she turned sad and quietness settled over her now normally buoyant personality, Bradford understood and held his arms out to her. And if she turned morose and introspective, concerned her past would somehow harm this wonderful, supportive man, he'd get down and dirty with tickling fingers and a pounding with the sole intent of taking her mind from her troubles.

At least for a little while.

"I love you, Bradford Lynden," Fay whispered against her husband's throat.

"I love you, too," Bradford mumbled.

"They're gonna find him, Brad."

"Yes, they are."

"What if he won't…?"

"Don't borrow trouble, Fay-Fay," her husband said.

She closed her eyes and settled closer still to her rock, her anchor, the love of her life. When sleep finally overcame her, she dreamt she was standing at the kitchen sink of the shabby little trailer to which she had brought her son all those years before. She was bathing the little boy, laughing with him, being splattered by his flailing arms as he tried to grab the rubber ducky floating in the sink beside his chubby leg. As she gently washed his tiny genitals, she smiled at the odd little birthmark on the puckered flesh of his scrotum.

"That's gonna intrigue a lady one day, Paddy," she said, picking him up and wrapping the towel around his squirming little body.

She carried her son to the bed and dressed him in his nightie then sat down in the old rocking chair to croon him to sleep.

Deep in her slumber, her face pressed against Bradford's chest, Fay O'Reilly Lynden heard the song she was singing to her child and tears slid from the corners of her eyes.

Chapter Three

Julian St. John stood at the sweeping bank of windows that looked out over the docks and waited for the arrival of his clients. The yacht bearing Dr. Olivia Carstairs, her assistant and two women who were new to the resort was dropping anchor as the sun sank below the horizon. He blinked as the lights on the dock came on, illuminating the crewmen who began scurrying about to secure the craft.

His assistant, Henri Bouvier, went through the rundown of the new clients and pairing suggestions. Julian asked, "And the woman with Olivia? Who is she?" He was staring at the woman in question as she stood on the dock and seemed to be admiring his personal yacht *The Connemara*, anchored at the end of the quay. Clearly distracted, she didn't notice her camera bags slipping down her arms. He saw the moment she knew they were going to fall and watched with interest and an amusement he rarely felt as she fumbled to gather her belongings. She reminded him of an ingénue in the middle of Times Square gawking at the bright lights. There was a sweetness about her that he never saw here at Mistral Cay. All of his clients were self-possessed and often selfish. Dr. Carstairs's assistant seemed to be a guppy swimming among sharks.

Henri consulted his notes. "Her name is Sara Trevor. She has been with Dr. Carstairs for six months and has the doctor's complete trust. She is here to take photographs of our helpers' genitalia."

Julian raised his brow in query.

"For Dr. Carstairs's book on the subject." Henri turned a page in the binder he was carrying. "The publisher will be Villiers and Dunst who specialize in medical school textbooks."

"What do you know of her?"

"Trevor?" At Julian's nod, Henri ran his finger down the report until he found the information. "Unmarried and unattached. A workaholic by Dr. Carstairs's estimate. Lives alone. Has a cat named Xander. She is a graduate of Northwestern with a degree in sociology. Has won several photographic awards, mostly for her abstracts. She is here strictly as Dr. Carstairs's assistant and doesn't wish to take part in any programs offered by the resort."

"Really?" Julian muttered. His attention was glued to the women disembarking the yacht. With a practiced eye, he identified the new clients and made adjustments to their pairings.

Olivia Carstairs was the next to pass over the gangplank. She looked up at the bank of windows and waved, knowing Julian would be on hand to view the newcomers.

"Dr. Carstairs has asked for you again," Henri sighed. "She doesn't give up, does she?"

"One of these days she just might get what she's wishing for," Julian said softly. "Who did you assign to her?"

"Frederick. She likes him well enough. He's put in for a three-week leave after her departure. I okayed it since he always seems to need R and R after one of her visits."

Julian narrowed his eyes as the fourth woman stepped onto the gangplank. He stared at her for a moment then stepped over to the computer monitor showing the closed-circuit camera view of the arrivals and reached for the mouse, clicking on the magnification icon to zoom in on Sara Trevor's face.

And what a lovely face, Julian thought as his gaze moved over the young woman's features. A pert, slightly upturned nose, high cheekbones, sultry lips and a determined chin gave sensuality to her pixie face. Her small yet athletic frame held shapely curves beneath her short-sleeve pullover and tapered slacks. Her slender arms held his attention and caused a slight stirring he had not experienced in his groin in quite some time. While clearly out of her element, she surprised him with her self-assurance in the way she moved, unconscious class in her stride and command in her body language as she spoke to Dr. Carstairs. He watched her until she was out of the camera's range.

"I will interview Miss Trevor," Julian said quietly.

"She doesn't wish to participate in—"

"Bring her to me tomorrow morning."

Henri inclined his head, knowing better than to argue with his boss. What Julian wanted, Julian always received. "As you wish."

"And give her the Forest Suite," Julian ordered.

Henri looked up from his writing. "You will be handling this personally?"

"Yes," Julian replied in a low voice. "This one is mine."

* * * * *

Kiley had never seen anything to match the suite to which she was shown. The parlor had exquisite dark oak furnishings complimented by a delicate floral print on the twin loveseats, occasional chairs and the fabulous chaise lounge that beckoned a try. Glass-top tables with carved bases made to look like woodland creatures made up the desk and chair side tables. A vast armoire held the entertainment center where several hundred CDs and DVDs were housed.

"The sleeping area is through here," the bellman said, holding the door open for Kiley.

Upon entering the sleeping area, her mouth dropped open, her eyes flared wide and she could not seem to find her voice. As the bellman rattled on about room service and the other amenities available at the resort, she stood stock still, marveling at the most remarkable bed she'd ever seen.

Soaring over a king-sized mattress set higher than normal from the floor was a headboard that resembled an ancient gnarled tree. The two-foot-thick trunk rose up from the carpet in one twisted column, resembling an ages-old oak sliced in twain. With sweeping branches fanned out along the wall and arched over the mattress, the intricately carved wood was dotted with silk leaves in myriad shades of green with a few yellow, orange and red leaves to make them appear lifelike. The leaves moved gently in the light breeze coming from a pair of opened French doors and made a soft rustling sound. The coverlet spread over the bed gave the illusion there was a bed of flowers growing beneath the knotted oak.

The only fixture in the room, the bed was set at an angle to two walls done in a spectacular forest scene with rolling hills and a silver-shot stream rambling between lush green banks. The room smelled of a mixture of wisteria and gardenia, and upon closer inspection, those heady plants had been painted along a rustic fence in the mural. The third wall contained the French doors and the fourth was covered in mirrored panels up and down its entire expanse, the reflection of the mural making the forest scene go on as though forever.

Kiley walked over to the bed and ran her hand along the coverlet. The sensuous feel of the material made her sigh.

"Does the room meet with your satisfaction, Miss Trevor?" the bellman inquired.

Dragging her gaze from the beautiful floral pattern, Kiley nodded. She started to open her shoulder bag to tip the bellman but the handsome young man held up a hand.

"Everything is included in the price of the room, ma'am," he said.

"Wow," was all Kiley could manage to say.

"Dinner will be in a half hour in the Sea Crest Room. If you prefer, room service is available twenty-four hours a day. I highly recommend the lobster Florentine."

"Thank you," Kiley replied. She craned her head to read the bellman's name badge. "Steve."

"My pleasure, ma'am."

She looked around, but before she could ask, the bellman touched one of the mirrored panels on the wall. A hidden door opened with a low click, revealing a huge walk-in closet with built-in dressers.

"The second panel from the left is the bathing suite," the bellman said with a smile.

"Wow," Kiley said again as he pushed against the panel behind which the bathing suite was located.

"Would you like me to unpack for you?"

"Oh, no," Kiley was quick to say. "I'll do it." She had always hated other people handling her personal belongings.

"Well, if there is nothing else, I'll be going. If there is anything you need, anything at all, please ask for me."

"What room is Dr. Carstairs in?"

"I believe she is in her usual room," he replied. "The Regal Suite."

Kiley smiled. "That sounds like her."

"Each of the rooms has a theme," the bellman said. "If you get a chance, take a stroll by the Lagoon suite. It is truly breathtaking. There is an aquarium arced over the bed in that room."

Kiley whistled. "That I gotta see."

Steve bowed slightly and let himself out, gently closing the thick, carved oak door behind him.

Looking about her, Kiley walked to the bathing suite and poked her head in. The sight that greeted her made her eyes go wide. If the headboard of the bed had surprised her, the bathing suite stunned her even more.

Besides a long vanity holding dual marble sinks, there was a toilet and bidet, a vast walk-in glass shower with a marble seating shelf and showerheads on three sides, and a well-appointed dressing table. But the piece de resistance was the huge spa tub in pale green marble with delicate white veining that took center stage in the plush chamber. Sunken into the tile floor and sitting at the base of floor-to-ceiling mullioned windows that gave a magnificent view of the ocean beyond, the tub looked so inviting Kiley couldn't wait to climb inside and turn the brass jets on full force.

Biting her lip, she was trying to decide if she wanted to dress for supper or simply call room service for a light snack. The tub was calling out to her and the thought of sinking beneath the swirling waters was too tempting to pass up. She knew the next few days would be embarrassing at the least, humiliating at the most, and having the rest of this evening to herself to relax and drive all thoughts of her assignment from her mind, seemed too important to ignore.

She turned away from the tub and headed for the parlor, but the bed snared her attention and she made a detour. Kicking off her shoes, she heaved herself onto the mattress then gave a loud sigh of contentment as she sank into the marshmallow feel of it. Without another thought, she stretched out, allowing her body to become enveloped in the soft but firm surface.

"Oh, man," she whispered, reveling in the sensation the mattress was causing. It was almost like floating on air, no pressure points to feel along her back and legs. "I'm gonna sleep good tonight."

For ten minutes she laid there, the magic mattress relaxing her more than she could ever remember feeling in her life. It took a great deal of willpower to get up and go into the other room for the room-service menu. All she really wanted to do was lie there until morning but her tummy was growling and she knew she'd come down with a hunger headache if she didn't eat.

The food descriptions looked wonderful, which made her choices exceedingly difficult. By the time she picked up the receiver and dialed room service, her mouth was beginning to water.

With her order made, Kiley reclined once more on the soft, encompassing bed and closed her eyes. The sweet scent of gardenia wafted under her nostrils and she sighed deeply.

When the discreet knock came at her door, she hated to get up. Struggling to push her way from the seductive mattress, she padded barefoot to the parlor door and opened it with a slight smile that froze in place as she stared at the room-service attendant.

He was tall—well over six feet—with a naked chest full of curling black hair that accentuated six-pack abs and chiseled pecs. His bulging biceps flexed as he stood there with her tray in his strong-looking hands. The black silk britches covering his long legs and narrow hips molded to him like a second skin. Barefoot, he was standing with those long legs spread in a posture that was sensuous and threatening at the same time.

"Ah, would you put the tray on the table?" Kiley asked, stepping back. Her gaze was locked on the silk mask tied around the top part of his face, hiding his hair and nose yet calling attention to piercing eyes that seemed to look straight into her soul.

His derriere was curved nicely high and looked rock-hard as he walked past her. Broad shoulders enveloped in a golden tan tapered down to a slim waist, hugged lovingly by the elastic band holding up the britches. The pull of the silk britches against his taut thighs and hips made her want to run her hands down his legs. As he bent over to place the tray on the table by the windows, she drew in a slow breath as the fabric molded itself to his lean posterior. When he turned to face her, his hands hanging loosely at his sides, the thick bulge at the juncture of his legs drew her immediate attention. It was all she could do to drag her eyes from that enticing sight. The only visible mark on that superb body had been a long, upwardly slanting scar on his back just under his left rib cage. Having seen a similar scar on a client, she wondered if this gorgeous specimen had been the giver or recipient of a donated kidney.

"Thank you," she said, wishing she had a name for this delectable hunk.

A slight bow of his head was his acknowledgement of her gratitude. He seemed to be waiting for any instructions she might have and when she remained silent, he started toward her, his dark eyes glistening behind the slits of the mask.

Kiley had the urge to place her hands against that hairy chest and waylay this mysterious man. Her palms actually itched from the mental push to do just that and she had to rub them down her slacks to wipe away the moisture gathering there. Unconsciously, she licked her upper lip as he passed. At the door, he turned, his head cocked to one side as though in question.

"Ah, no," she whispered then had to clear her throat and speak louder. "No, that will be all."

He seemed to sigh, his wide chest rising and falling in a brief movement that set Kiley's breasts to tingling. With one final bow of his head, he left the room, leaving behind an aura that brought a flush to her face and set her juices to flowing between her legs.

"Damn," she whispered. She had a feeling she was going to be sorry she'd chosen not to participate in the pleasures of Mistral Cay.

Chapter Four

Julian peeled the mask from his face and pulled on a shirt as he positioned himself behind the middle panel of the two-way mirror that looked into the bedroom of the Forest Suite. From the moment Henri had told him about the Trevor woman Julian had been suspicious of her. She had an agenda beyond the one she'd given. In order to make sure she posed no threat to him personally, he needed to find out what he could about her. Spying on her when she was unaware was a damned good way of discovering hidden agendas and secrets. Perhaps she'd call someone. Muse aloud to herself. Give him some idea of just what she was really doing on his island.

He took up state-of-the-art headphones and positioned them over his head, adjusting the sound on a dial just over his left ear. The space in which he stood was situated between the suite's bathing area and walk-in closet. It was little more than three feet in width, the walls covered with soundproof panels, the ceiling and floor padded. The only light in the space came from a nineteen-inch flat-screen monitor showing a view from the parlor. Below the monitor was a built-in shelf that held a keyboard and mouse. With a click, he zoomed in on the occupant of the suite as she took a seat at the table and began eating the supper he had brought her.

He studied her every movement as she brought spoon or fork to her lips, wiped delicately at her mouth with the linen napkin from the tray or nibbled at her sandwich. His amber gaze narrowed as she sipped the peach wine, his groin tightening when she put out her tongue to lick her upper lip.

She was beautiful with shoulder-length blonde tresses drawn back in a no-nonsense ponytail. Though she wore no makeup, her face required none, for the color of her green eyes framed in long dark lashes, ripe coral lips and sun-kissed cheeks drew the eye better than any artificial enhancement ever could. Her beauty was natural, unpolished like an uncut gem waiting for the right hand to touch it.

"Julian?"

The sound from the tiny microphone startled him and he frowned, annoyed with the intrusion. "Yes," he snapped softly into the foam-covered mouthpiece arched in front of his lips.

"I'm sorry to bother you but I knew you would be interested in the news from Des Moines," Henri Bouvier told him.

"Tell me."

"As you suspected, the lady in question is not the good doctor's assistant nor is she a graduate of Northwestern. She is, in fact, a private investigator hired to locate a client's son here on the Cay."

Julian caught his breath but before he could ask, Henri set his mind at ease.

"It's not your mother, Julian. The client is a woman named Fay Lynden."

Letting out a long breath, Julian closed his eyes. "Who is the man she's looking for?"

"That name is not yet known, I'm afraid."

"Why not?"

"Mrs. Lynden was sent to prison when the boy was a toddler. He was adopted and she does not know by whom. We are tracing that now."

"And this Sara Trevor was hired to find the woman's son," Julian stated.

"Actually, Ms. Trevor's real name is Kiley," Henri said, amusement rife in his New Orleans accent.

Watching the woman get up from the table and come into the bedroom, Julian thought the name appropriate for a female who moved so sensually. It wasn't an exotic name but it fit her.

"Is there a Xander?" he asked. Mention of the cat Sara Trevor supposedly owned elicited a chuckle from Henri.

"Yes, there is a Xander. He's an orange and white Maine Coon. I believe her neighbor is quoted as saying the cat is the love of her life."

"A silky feline for a silky female," Julian quipped. "Boyfriend? Husband?"

"Neither."

"Seeing anyone on a regular basis?"

"Not for several years."

"Why's she wanting to look at strange men's pricks, then?"

"You're going to like this—she's looking for a birthmark."

There was a short pause then Julian whispered, "Say again."

"The man she's looking for has a birthmark on his balls." When Julian made no reply to his answer, Henri said, "If I hear anything else, I'll let you know immediately."

"Not tonight," Julian ordered. Before hearing the confirmation from his assistant that his order would be followed, Julian peeled the microphone from his head and hooked it on the wall beside the monitor.

The object of his surveillance was unbuttoning her blouse when Julian turned his attention to the two-way mirror again. Bracing his hands to either side of the two-foot-wide panel, he stood there watching as she slid the blouse from her slender shoulders and tossed it on the bed. The light beige teddy that covered her upper body was trimmed in pale green lace that matched the color of her eyes. As her fingers moved to the waistband of her slacks, tugging down the side zipper, his breathing increased. When she pushed the slacks down her shapely legs and stepped out of them, he could hear the rush of blood in his ears.

Losing sight of her as she walked into the bathing suite, he clenched his jaw and turned back to the monitor. His hand went to the mouse, moving the cursor to the tub icon on the taskbar. He felt like an obsessed stalker as he eagerly waited for the camera to find her again.

"There you are," he said quietly and felt a strange sensation in the region of his heart.

Relief? Yes, that was exactly what it was. Relief mixed in with a great big helping of protectiveness.

The feelings surprised the hell out of him, until he realized there was another emotion trying to break out of its hard-encased shell. An emotion he had never experienced before. One he'd ruthlessly tamped down all of his life. An emotion that made you weak, but one he was beginning to realize was something he desperately needed.

"Get that shit right out of your head, St. John. It's not for you."

He wasn't the kind of man this woman needed. Or should have. He was damaged goods, ruined, and so far beneath her, a decent, sweet woman but…

The more he watched her—unable to look away though he felt like as low as the slimy belly of a slug—the more he wanted what her dewy freshness advertised. He was stunned to find he was equating her with white picket fences with a rose-covered trellis arched above a flagstone path leading to a shadowed front porch. He put his hand on the two-way glass and felt like a little boy looking into a candy store window.

She was bending over the faucets, turning the water on in the spa tub as the hidden camera in the ceiling tracked her movements. Dissatisfied with the angle, Julian moved the feed to other cameras until he was looking at her beautiful face. He zoomed in on her face, held by the dreamy, expectant expression that had softened her features. When she raised her hands to pull down first one strap of the teddy then the other, he could feel the sweat forming on his upper lip. Though the space in which he stood was air conditioned, he felt as though he had been thrust into the gaping maw of an oven.

Passion, he thought, as he became aware of his hand shaking, especially passion so long denied, could turn a man into a ravaging beast and that was the thought running through his mind as he watched Kiley Trevor peel the teddy from her luscious body. What he saw brought a low growl of need roaring up from the very core of him.

Her breasts were dewy perfect with large areolas tinted a succulent deep rose. As she lifted her arms to pull the band from her ponytail, those breasts were firm and high with no telltale surgical lines. The globes were like a siren call beckoning him to explore their creamy smoothness. He could almost taste the duskiness of the small, hard nipples and ached to run his tongue over the puckered flesh.

Fire invaded his loins as she squatted down beside the tub. His finger automatically lowered the camera view—zooming in on the shadow at the juncture of her legs. The view lasted only a second but it had been long enough for him to get a glimpse of a neatly trimmed bush that stoked the fire of his lust even higher. He fancied he could smell the heat of her and his nostrils quivered like that of a wild beast.

Watching her slide gracefully into the water that was now bubbling fiercely from the jets, he reached up with his left hand to rub at the headache that was forming in his temple. The tightness in his head mirrored the straining tightness beneath the black silk britches, the front of which was slick with the fluid of building passion.

She moved so languidly, obviously enjoying the feel of the warm water caressing her body. The loofah she dragged along her arms, across her chest, from side to side over her belly seemed to give her great pleasure, for her eyes were closed and a slight smile played over her sultry lips. As she brought first one leg then the other up to run the fibrous sponge down them, she opened her eyes and appeared to sigh. When she finished with her legs, she lay her head back along the cushioned pad behind her and closed her eyes once more, apparently just lying there experiencing the tumble and heat of the water, relaxed and serene.

"Enjoy the serenity while you can, sweetness," Julian whispered, reaching down to rub at the swelling between his legs. "I intend to make this assignment as difficult for you as I can. Then you need to leave here and never come back. You're a complication I can't afford."

He was about to turn away, to leave her to the rest of her bath but when she lowered the loofah beneath the water, he stilled, instinct telling him to leave would be to miss something exquisite.

There was no mistaking the motion below the tumbling waves. Nor could there have been any doubt as to the intent of Kiley Trevor's actions. Her lips were slightly parted, her eyes still closed, a slight puckering between her brows as she concentrated on pleasuring herself.

"God," Julian breathed. Completely ensnared by what he was seeing, he slid his hand down the front of his britches to grip his cock, his fingers spanned beneath it, his thumb flexed on the coronal ridge. He began to move his hand back and forth on his engorged member as Kiley Trevor reached up to pluck at the nipple of her right breast.

His breathing increasing, he slid his other hand into his trousers and gripped the end of his cock, sliding his thumb and index finger in a tight coil around the head of his throbbing shaft. Working alternately left then right, he rotated the head of his cock, twisting slowly at first but as he watched Kiley pleasuring herself, his action increased in speed and in the tightness with which he held the tip of his cock. He envisioned his tool sliding into her creamy channel, tightening around him, bringing a wet, wild sensation of intense satisfaction to his rock-hard shaft. Heat flared through his lower body and he could feel sweat popping out on his upper lip and in the center of his chest. He could smell the ripe aroma of his pre-cum and he imagined the musky scent of Kiley's cunt drifting to him from the steaming water in which she now reclined. His heart was racing, his breathing ragged as his hand moved faster and faster, pulling, twisting, elongating his shaft while at the same time pressing his other hand hard against his belly and his pelvic region.

He was on fire with a need he had not felt in many years. It wasn't just the relief he knew he had needed for so long but the sensual woman pleasuring herself in the room beyond that made his blood sing and his cock throb with a life of its own. He stared at her half-closed eyes—memorizing her beautiful face, letting his fevered gaze slide over her luxurious breasts. He ached to touch them, to suckle them, to draw the rosy tips deep into his mouth, to scrape his teeth lightly across them until she was writhing beneath him in complete abandonment, her body his to enjoy, to pleasure, to possess.

"Kiley," he whispered and the rhythm of his hand increased in direct proportion to the rubbing of the loofah between her thighs. He could not take his eyes from her dewy face and as he did, he saw the exact moment her passion became full blown. He was but a step behind her, his own face mirroring the depth of the pleasure that came roaring up to claim him.

Their orgasms came at the same instant, stunning Julian as he stood there quivering from head to toe, his knees so weak he had to lean against the wall to steady himself. His breathing was as ragged as hers, their hands trembling as they reached in tandem to push away a stray lock of sweat-dampened hair from their foreheads.

Those dual actions were like a sign to Julian St. John. He took them for the omens he had long sought.

He shouldn't be spying on her. It was wrong and it was something he'd never done before. The Forest Suite was for those who wanted to experience the voyeuristic side of sex. He'd never had the urge to spy on people making love. Being a peeping Tom wasn't him, didn't interest him, but he couldn't stop watching this woman. He wanted to know everything there was to know about her. What made her tick. What she liked. What she disliked. What she wanted from life.

What turned her on.

He wanted to turn her on.

"You will be mine, sweetness," Julian vowed, his eyes locked on hers as though she could see through the hidden camera lens into his secret place. "No matter what else I do to you, you will be mine."

He wanted her. God, how he wanted her. A taste—if nothing more. He knew she wasn't for him. He sure as hell didn't deserve a woman like her but he was drawn to her like a moth to flame. Tearing himself away from his spying was proving to be impossible.

Long into the night he watched her from the mini-cam hidden in a branch of the headboard. He kept vigil over her supple body as she lay naked on the floral coverlet. He watched the delicate rise and fall of her chest, smiled at the movement of her eyes as she dreamt, ached as he stared at the glistening pelt over her mound. By the time he tore himself away and staggered lust-drunk from his observation space, he was once more a lonely man sorely in need of a mate.

In some deep, hidden part of his mind was a thought he had always refused to let surface. An ache in his heart he refused to acknowledge before now. He wanted that white picket fence. He wanted the latticework trellis with the roses climbing over it. He wanted the shadowed front porch with a couple of white rocking chairs: one for him and one for…

"Kiley," he said, and some part of his damaged psyche admitted what he dared not say aloud.

He was losing his black heart to a woman he knew he should leave the hell alone.

But—he thought as he tossed the covers of his bed back—what if he could show her the man behind the façade? What if he could introduce her to the real man buried deep inside him? Would it be possible for her to fall for him as he was surely falling for her?

As he climbed into bed, he looked at the bedside clock, and without giving himself time to back out, he grabbed the phone and dialed a number he hadn't called in eighteen years. Never once doubting the number would have changed, he held the receiver tightly to his ear as the transatlantic call went through.

"Bellington residence," a stiff voice with a proper English accent announced.

"I'd like to speak with Mrs. Bellington," Julian said, his jaw clenched.

"May I ask who is calling?"

"It's me, Guildford. It's Anthony."

"Oh," the voice on the other end said, dropping the word like a hot brick. "One moment, sir."

Guildford had been with the family for as long as Julian could remember. A prim and proper gentleman who wore his rank with impeccable stiffness, Guildford was incapable of smiling—or so it had seemed to Julian as he was growing up.

"Anthony? Oh, my dear boy," his mother shrieked. "Where are you? How are you?"

"I'm fine, Mother," he replied. "How are you?"

"Oh, Anthony." He heard her crying, sniffling, and knew she would be carrying a delicate lace handkerchief to wipe her eyes. "Why haven't you called? I have been so worried. I—"

"Mother, do you remember the words to the Connemara Cradle Song?" Julian interrupted. He held his breath, waiting for her answer.

There was a long pause. "Whatever are you talking about?"

"The lullaby, Mother. Do you remember singing it to me when I was a child?"

"Anthony, my word," she said. "I couldn't carry a tune in a hand basket. Why are you asking me such a thing?"

"Did Margaret sing it to me?"

"I suppose she might have. I don't recall. What do you—?"

"Is she there?"

"Heavens, no," his mother stated. "She's been dead ten years or so. There was an accident with a lorry. Very horrible affair as it were. Why on earth would you want to talk to a servant? You haven't called your own mother in all these years and now you—"

"I have to go, Mother," Julian said. "I'm glad you're all right."

"Anthony? You wait just a minute. Your Uncle Clive wants to speak with you. He—"

The unmistakable sound of the phone being grabbed away from his mother made Julian lower the receiver.

"Anthony. Anthony, answer me!" His uncle's voice was strident, as hateful as he remembered the man being.

Replacing the receiver, cutting off the detested voice, Julian turned over in the bed and pulled his pillow to him. The scar on his back began to burn and he reached behind him to massage the puckered flesh.

When he had fled the English estate on which he had grown up, he had tried to shed the painful memories as easily as he had shed the name Anthony Lanier James Bellington. The memories, however, could not be dismissed as easily as he had hoped, though he had spent half a lifetime trying to forget his childhood.

He loved his mother as much as he had hated his father and feared his uncle. Not seeing her, not talking to her had been beyond difficult, but that was the only way he could stay safe and out of the clutches of a family that had nearly destroyed him.

Chapter Five

"But I won't be participating in the programs offered here at the resort," Kiley protested to Henri Bouvier. "Why do I need to be interviewed by Mr. St. John?"

"You may not wish to indulge in the pleasures offered here, Ms. Trevor," Bouvier replied, "but you will be utilizing resort personnel. Mr. St. John wants to make sure your presence here is…shall we say? Kosher?"

Kiley frowned. "Why wouldn't it be kosher, Mr. Bouvier? I am here as Dr. Carstairs's assistant and—"

"If you wish to stay at the Cay and perform your duties as the good doctor's assistant, then you must meet with Mr. St. John and acquire his approval," Henri interrupted in a firm, no-argument tone.

Letting out an annoyed breath, Kiley put her hands on her hips, lowered her head in defeat and sighed again. "All right," she said, looking up. "But I don't see the need."

Henri shrugged. "It isn't up to us to question his orders, Ms. Trevor. I learned long ago not to do that."

Irritated even more by Bouvier's subservient attitude, Kiley pursed her lips. The more she heard about St. John, the less inclined she was to meet with him. That his manner was one of a despot, a dictator of this tropical paradise did not set well with her. Added to that impression of him, his method of carving out an empire for himself by selling male flesh to wealthy, bored women made him little more than an expensive pimp to her way of thinking.

"All right," she said again. "Let's get it over with then."

Henri frowned.

Tough, huh? Kiley thought. Apparently, a woman unwilling to meet with the great Julian St. John was a rarity. If other women fell all over themselves and couldn't wait to be ushered into the presence of the infamous lord of Mistral Cay, say hello to the woman who didn't. Men who felt entitled had always rubbed her the wrong way. She didn't like the superior attitudes and she suspected a man like St. John would have a brutal ego and pompous sense of self-importance.

"Fine," she said under her breath. She'd meet with *his lordship* and slap him down a peg or two. Let him know she didn't appreciate his highhanded ways.

"Please follow me," Henri said, his scowl deepening as he heard Kiley's exaggerated sigh of displeasure.

She barely glanced at the luxurious accoutrements they passed on the way to St. John's office. The investigator part of her nature noted the beautifully carved panels of teak, the heavy gold damask drapes, the clearly expensive paintings gracing the walls and the exquisite fabrics on the seating arrangements. She took in the thick carpet underfoot, the pleasant smell of wisteria hanging in the air, the coolness of the wide hallway down which they moved, the lambent light that cast lush shadows from the tall potted palms they passed. While such trappings impressed her, she needed to maintain a mien of being unaffected by the display of the vast wealth and discriminating taste.

Henri stopped before a wide double door, the surface of which was carved with a scene similar to that in the murals in Kiley's bedroom. He reached up to straighten his tie before knocking and Kiley wondered why a man would dress so formally at what was tantamount to a male brothel. This morning's entertainment included watching several guests and their helpers frolicking naked at the beach. Held captive by the sight of deeply tanned masculine male bodies, she had forgotten breakfast to watch the revelers. Her stomach reminded her of that oversight just as a deep masculine voice called, "Come" from beyond the door.

Bouvier reached for the brass handle and swung the door open, stepping aside to allow Kiley to enter. She glanced up at him, realizing he was not going to accompany her, and squared her shoulders.

"In for a penny, in for a pound," she mumbled to herself and entered St. John's lair.

At first she thought she was in the room alone. It was a beautifully designed office with a huge mahogany desk behind which stood a wide burgundy leather chair, its rounded back to her. Behind the desk was a sweeping bank of windows that looked out over the ocean. In front of the desk was a comfortable looking club chair done in a lovely jacquard pattern of rose, teal and pale yellow.

"Please have a seat, Ms. Trevor."

Kiley was further bothered by the man's lack of manners. He was sitting with his back to her, ostensibly, staring out the windows.

She clasped her hands in her lap and decided she would be just as blasé about this so-called interview as was he.

"Tell me," he said, still not turning around, "what do you call the midline seam that runs along the underside of a man's shaft, Ms. Trevor?"

Kiley blinked. "I beg your pardon?"

"Is it the frenulum?" he queried. "The seminal vesicles?"

He swung his chair around. "Or is it the jaculum?"

Kiley found herself staring into a face that was by far the most handsome she had ever seen; a purely masculine face with bold eyebrows that arched over eyes the color of dark topaz. Sensuous lips—the bottom fuller than the top—were perfectly framed beneath high cheekbones and a nose that would be a plastic surgeon's dream. Strong, even white teeth, ears that were positioned perfectly against St. John's head over which a thick mane of sleek black hair curled in careless abandon and an athletic neck that suggested a youthful regimen of bridging exercises cast an undeniable picture of health, vitality and male supremacy. Only his jawline hinted at a nature that could be rife with danger.

"Well?" he prodded. "Which is it?"

Kiley cleared her throat. "I don't have a clue what a jaculum is, but the midline seam that runs on the underside of your penis, Mr. St. John, is called the raphe."

St. John smiled and that smile sent a tremor down Kiley's spine.

"And the seminal vesicles?" he asked.

Glad for the crash course in penal anatomy Dr. Carstairs had given her on the plane trip to the Cay, Kiley relaxed in her chair, crossing one leg over the other.

"They are on the sides of the scrotal sac. They feel like little twigs." She arched a brow. "And what, pray tell, is a jaculum?"

St. John's smile widened. "Perhaps I meant ejaculum," he responded.

"Well, if that's what you meant, that's just another word for cum, Mr. St. John. Cum is—"

"I know what it is, Ms. Trevor," he said, cutting her off.

Kiley lifted her chin. "I'm sure you do," she said.

He made a steeple with his fingers and rested the tips beneath his chin as he braced his elbows on the chair arms. "How many—

would you estimate—cocks have you photographed for Dr. Carstairs?"

She could feel the blush creeping into her cheeks and from the knowing look in his stare, she knew he could see the telltale color. Realizing he was watching her intently, ready to pounce on a lie, she shrugged. "None as of yet."

"Really?" he asked. "But you do know what you're looking for?"

There was no mistaking the twinkle in his eye and although she wasn't sure if he was teasing or goading her, she cocked her head to one side.

"Well, let's see—hopefully a long, fleshy piece of cartilage with a bush of crinkly pubic hair on top and a heavy scrotum hanging beneath. Some will be circumcised and some won't. If they are, the head of the shaft will be apparent. If not, it will be necessary to have the subject pull—"

"I believe you know what you're looking for," he said, amusement turning his eyes a lighter shade of gold.

"Yeppers, I do," she said brightly. "Cocks of all different sizes and shapes and colors and—"

"When would you like to start?" he interrupted harshly.

She was taken aback by his strident tone and slightly unnerved by the sudden hardening of his features.

"Will I have access to the resort grounds or will you send the men to me to photograph?" she asked.

His gaze narrowed. "Which do you prefer?"

Though it was a lie, she said she had to admit she would like to see what the resort was like. In truth, she didn't want to be alone in a room with a man whose penis was only inches from her face. Out in the open, with others around, seemed a bit less intimidating although she feared it would be more embarrassing.

He stared at her for a long moment then leaned back in his chair. "I will have Henri find a spot for you on the beach. At any given time there are always helpers around. Do you have a preference of what size or shape or color you'd like to start with?"

She wished she could tell him she needed to see only the penises of those men who were white and thirty-seven years of age but then he would know she was there for a purpose other than what had been put forth.

"I'll leave that up to you," she said, ducking her head and pretending to flick lint from her cotton skirt.

"Unless it is in the fantasy scenario, the helpers are not allowed to speak with the guests," he said. "Since you have opted not to participate in the pleasures offered at the Cay, the men will not answer any questions you put to them, so don't bother trying."

Kiley's eyebrows shot up. "Not even Steve?" she inquired. "You know, the bellboy?"

Julian St. John's eyes narrowed. "I know who the hell Steve is."

"Since he and I have already spoken can't I—?"

"Steven is not one of the helpers, but if you would like to photograph his cock, feel free," Julian snapped. He got up from the chair. "If you want to question him about the size and shape and color of his prick, by all means do so. I'm sure he'd love to tell you all about it."

With that, the owner of Mistral Cay skirted the desk and strode angrily to the door, slamming the portal shut behind him.

Kiley sat there for a moment her head swiveled toward the closed door. She was stunned by both St. John's abrupt manner as well as the fury she had glimpsed in his molten glower. It was almost as though he was exhibiting jealousy, male possessiveness, but since she did not know him, had never met him before today, she knew that could not be the cause of his obvious anger. He certainly couldn't be enamored of her on such short acquaintance unless…

Unless Steve is his lover, she thought.

That notion didn't sit well with her and she slumped in the chair, considering it. Anything was possible, but she hated thinking he batted for the other team.

With that sobering thought, she left his office without slamming the door.

* * * * *

"Give Steve Bertran a couple of weeks off," Julian ordered Henri. "All expenses paid to Miami or L.A. or wherever the fuck the little shit wants to go."

Henri knew better than to ask why. He simply made a notation in the book he was never seen without. "When would you like me to start sending helpers to Ms. Trevor?"

"You've picked a spot?" Julian snapped.

"As you suggested, it is within full view of the cabanas. I have provided a small tent and have had her equipment set up."

"Equipment never used before now," Julian said with a snort.

"The price tags were still on two of the lenses."

Another vicious snort came from Julian. "Did you place the call as I asked?" he demanded.

Henri sighed heavily. "Julian, don't I always do as you ask?"

Julian ignored the question. "Have the helpers meet with me in about twenty minutes. If you need to pull them from a scenario, do it."

Such an order was outside the norm and Henri winced. "Julian, won't that be impinging on the ladies' entertainment? I mean—"

"Don't argue with me, Bouvier. Just do it."

Henri stiffened his posture. "As you wish." He clicked his heels together, turned with military precision and marched off, his back ramrod straight.

Julian ran a hand through his hair and tugged. He hated speaking to his best friend in such a manner but his nerves were beginning to get the best of him.

As was an acute jealousy that, until today, he had never experienced.

"Steve Bertran won't be showing you his wares, sweetness," he swore as he shoved his hands into the pockets of his black jeans.

Chapter Six

It wasn't as bad as she thought it was going to be. The first two sessions were clumsy attempts on her part to be in charge of the situation. No doubt sensing her nervousness and embarrassment, the first two young men came to stand before her in their youthful, nude glory and displayed their penises in a matter-of-fact manner. They held their members this way and that as she stammered her directions, lifted the shaft upward so she could photograph the scrotum, and at her expulsion of breath, lowered it for another photo or two before silently going on their way.

She began to relax after the third young man winked at her behind his mask as he strolled nonchalantly away, flexing his ass muscles for her benefit. Kiley laughed and wagged her finger at him when he glanced around at her. She heard his low chuckle as he trudged through the sand and went down to the water for a brief swim.

"I wonder who he really is," she mused to herself. "If he's someone I might know." Dr. Carstairs had told her some of the men who wore masks at the Cay were more than likely movie or television stars, even politicians biding their time at the Cay on a lark. Some even took a salary for their time spent there simply for the humor in it—certainly not because they needed it.

"Some of the women wear masks, too," Dr. Carstairs had commented. "They're well-respected matrons—many of them—and can't afford to have their identities known. Like people wouldn't recognize most of them the moment they open their mouths." She put a finger to her eye and pulled down the lower lid in a conspiratorial wink. "Of course, hiding behind a mask gives one the illusion of danger too, don't you think?"

It was the fourth specimen who ruined Kiley's complacent attitude.

From the moment she saw him striding toward her, she knew he was the man who had brought her supper the evening before. It would have been hard to forget those wide shoulders and narrow hips, the man's imposing height and masculine presence. Just watching him heading for her made her pulse quicken. She licked her lips, anxious to have him strip before her. Her gaze met his through his black silk mask and she thought she saw a gleam centered in his dark depths.

But then another man came into her line of vision and she flinched, looking up into the red leather-masked face with a frown. She was about to tell him to wait his turn but he stepped forward, his cock held like a weapon toward her.

Kiley recoiled, moving back. She glanced at the man from the night before and saw he had stopped twenty feet away and was just standing there, hands on his hips, feet apart, the black silk britches straining with the obvious bulge of his erection.

The man in front of her waggled his penis at her as though to gain her attention. It was an angry little thing with that one red-shot eye staring at her. If a penis could glare, this one was doing so for all it was worth. As short and stumpy as the pitiful little thing was, Kiley doubted it was worth much. When the man waggled it again, Kiley lost her temper.

"All right, already," she snapped. "Hold your horses, buster." She reached for her camera, hoping this wasn't the man for whom she was searching.

As she took her pictures, the man pulled his cock left to right and down, stretching the tiny thing as far as it would go—and that wasn't far. His shriveled balls were like withered prunes and then he lifted his penis upward.

"Thank God," Kiley said, spying no birthmark on the man's scrotal sac. She clicked one last picture she was sure was cockeyed and waved the man away.

There was a distinct snort from the young man as he hurried off.

"Bastard," Kiley pronounced and turned to the man from the night before.

He had not moved. He was standing in the exact same position, staring at her through the narrow slits of his mask. His chest was peppered with sweat from the hot sun beating down on him, though he didn't seem to care. As tan as his flesh was, he obviously was accustomed to the rays.

Kiley crooked her finger at him but he didn't move. Instead, he turned his head toward another young man coming toward the tent under which Kiley was sitting in her low-slung canvas chair.

"Oh, shit," Kiley said as the next man approached.

Though this man was built as beautifully as any naked man could be, he seemed to be deliberately hiding his scrotum from Kiley's view. When he lifted his penis upward, the bottom of his fist obscured the area she needed to see. When he shifted the penis from side to side, he once more covered the spot. After several attempts to get him to allow her full view of his scrotum, she finally had to say the words, "I need to see the scrotal sac, sir," her face turning bright red as he looked down at her, amusement glittering in his gaze.

Slowly, he cupped his member with his fingers, closing each one like an accordion over the swelling shaft. Even more slowly, he lifted his cock straight out and upward, arching his hips toward her so she could get a good look at his balls.

Kiley was only a foot away from the young man's family jewels and though they sparkled brightly, they were not the gems for which she was searching. She looked up and shook her head.

He stepped back as though stung by her reaction.

"Oh, no," she said, unthinkingly reaching out to grab his naked hips. "I just meant you weren't…I mean you aren't…" She felt the heat flowing down her neck. "You're quite nice but—"

He jerked out of her grip, lifted his head in the air and stomped off.

"Damn it," Kiley groaned. She hadn't meant to hurt the young man's feelings. She knew all too well how fragile was a man's ego when it came to his penis. She looked helplessly toward the man who was still watching her. He had not moved.

"I didn't mean to suggest he wasn't sexy," she called out. "He is way more man than I've seen in a long time but—"

The man from the night before stiffened, lowered his arms and turned his back to her. He, too, walked off as though she had insulted him. The white of the scar on his back was in livid contrast to the bronze of the rest of his tanned body.

"What the hell did I say?" she yelled and remembered Julian St. John telling her not to speak to the helpers except to tell them what to do.

Hot, angry, thirsty despite the bottles of spring water Henri Bouvier had provided for her in ice-filled tubs, Kiley threw her hands up and decided to call it quits. Five penises was enough work for one day.

"There are thirty helpers at the Cay," Dr. Carstairs had informed her.

"At this rate, it'll take me all week to inspect every cock here," Kiley mumbled to herself as she stomped through the hot sand. She was longing for that wonderful spa tub and a few Bloody Marias to make her forget all the sausages she'd been forced to stare at.

* * * * *

Julian slammed his fist against the doorframe hard enough to splinter the wood. Shaking his hand at the pain, cursing beneath his breath, he flopped down in his chair and thrust his long legs out in front of him.

"Devlin Parks is way more man than you've ever seen, eh?" he sneered, cradling his injured hand against his chest. "Well, baby, you ain't seen nothing yet."

* * * * *

"Steve is on vacation," the young man who served her supper informed her.

Kiley was disappointed. Not wanting to encounter Mr. Suppertime—as she had labeled him—she had decided against room service, although she would have preferred to eat alone in her room. She handed the menu back to the waiter. "I'll have the lobster Florentine."

"Excellent choice, Miss. And what kind of dressing for your salad?"

"Blue cheese and a carafe of white zinfandel with the meal."

"Certainly. I'll be right back with your wine."

Kiley smiled and looked around her. There were several other women dining in the Sea Crest Room that evening but none she had met, although one looked vaguely familiar. Since their arrival she had not seen Dr. Carstairs at all.

The waiter—his name was Trent—brought her wine and placed it before her; he spoke to her in a low voice.

"One of the helpers would like to join you for supper, Miss Trevor."

Kiley stared up at him. "One of the helpers?"

"He won't be eating with you but he has asked if he could sit with you while you ate."

"I don't know," Kiley said, surprised by the request. "I—"

She felt firm, gentle hands on her shoulders. The weight was heavy enough to be friendly but not possessive. The quick tensing of strong fingers, a gentle little pat, gave her the impression the man was greeting her in a lighthearted way.

Even before he came from behind her, softly dragging his fingertips across her upper back from shoulder to shoulder, she knew it would be him. She looked up and melted at the sight of him.

The silk mask was in place, hiding the color of his hair, but from the flesh tones of his hands and neck, she knew his hair would be dark, though perhaps not as dark as the black silk pirate shirt that fitted snuggly into the waistband of his black leather britches. The wiry hair revealed in the opening of the shirt and along the backs of his very capable-looking hands was dark brown.

"Do you always sit with the Cay's guests?" she asked as he took a seat beside her.

A careless shrug was his answer and she sighed, remembering the helpers were not allowed to speak to the women. She wanted to hear this man's voice for she knew it would be as sultry and seductive as the hot gleam in his amber eyes.

"I don't even know your name," she said as the waiter brought her salad.

"His name is Sean," the waiter said quietly as he placed the salad before her.

Kiley blushed. The waiter gave her a look that was knowing and amused. "Thank you," she mumbled.

"Sean is the most sought-after man at the Cay," the waiter continued. "He—"

There was a low growl from the man seated beside her and the waiter coughed, bowing curtly as he turned to leave. Kiley saw him glance back over his shoulder as though he expected her dining partner to come after him.

"Shame on you," she said. "Scaring away that perfectly good informer."

Sean chuckled behind the mask and when she looked into his eyes, she saw sheer deviltry staring back at her. This was a man who would bear watching, and remembering the way he had looked half-clothed on the beach that afternoon, she couldn't help but wonder what the rest of him looked like.

It was almost as though that thought had winged its way to the man in black for he reached out to take her hand in a light grip. As she watched—eyes wide and lips parted—he rubbed his thumb across the sensitive pulse point at her wrist and one golden eye closed slowly in an audacious wink.

Kiley jerked her hand out of his grasp, feeling the sensation of his fingertips to the depths of her womb. She looked down in her lap, took up her napkin and wiped at her mouth, though not one morsel of food or drink had passed her lips. She tucked the napkin back in her lap and hastily reached for her wine glass. She took a large gulp that seemed to amuse him if the sparkle in his tawny eyes was anything to go by.

"I'm not sure," she said, returning the wine glass to the table, "that I like you sitting there staring at me." She took up her fork and attacked her salad, chewing almost angrily as she glanced at him.

He cocked his head to one side then leaned back, folding his arms over his wide chest. The action made her mouth water more than the sweet-sour taste of the blue cheese dressing. His muscles strained against the shoulders of that luscious black shirt and those tapered fingers brought unbidden thoughts that made swallowing difficult.

"Does Mr. St. John know you are trying to seduce me?" she asked. When he nodded slowly, she paused with another forkful of salad halfway to her lips. She lowered the fork. "Even though I told him I didn't wish to participate in what the Cay offers?"

Once more he nodded slowly, the candlelight on the table reflecting across his black silk mask in a chevron pattern over his mesmerizing eyes.

"Well," Kiley said, "I think I need to speak with Mr. St. John. Obviously he doesn't listen well, but then, I'm not surprised; he is a rude man."

She hadn't meant her words to be insulting, but obviously Sean was offended. He unfolded his arms and stood in one graceful movement that made her reach out to him in apology.

"It's nothing to do with you," she said, taking that firm, strong wrist in her hand. She could feel the power of him, the heat of his flesh, and, heaven help her, she wanted to do things to him. Naughty things. "It's just that…I…well…" She trailed off, wanting yet not wanting the pleasures this man was offering. When he gently but firmly removed his hand from her grip, she groaned inwardly, her shoulders slumping.

He walked away, ignoring the women whose heads swiveled toward him as he passed.

"Idiot," Kiley named herself, appetite gone. She pushed the barely tasted salad away and shook her head.

It was going to be a long night, she thought as the waiter came toward her with the entrée.

* * * * *

He watched, again, as she pleasured herself in the big tub she couldn't seem to get enough of. "That could have been me inside you, sweetness," he whispered as he traced her arm on the monitor screen as she plied the loofah between her legs.

He was beginning to lose the last vestiges of shame he'd felt for spying on her. In his mind, she was already his and what she was doing in the tub was for his eyes alone. He decided to think of it as her way of enticing him, seducing him. He wanted her to seduce him. He wanted to feel her hands on him.

More than he had ever wanted any woman's hands on him—and he wanted his hands on her. To please her. To protect her and keep her out of harm's way.

Protect? Hell, he thought, he wasn't being protective. He was being possessive. He was beginning to look at her in a proprietary way that had confused him at first. Watching her on the beach as she photographed his workers had both amused and irritated him. The only cock he wanted her to observe was his own. He'd made a decision sometime during the afternoon—one that he had every intention of seeing come to fruition.

Kiley's eyes were closed and her neck arched gracefully against the tub's vinyl pillow. One leg was braced on the tub's rim, her prettily painted little toes arched as the friction from the loofah brought her close to satisfaction.

Standing it longer than he thought humanly possible, his breath coming in ragged gasps, he left his hiding place, tying the mask at the back of his head as he walked. In less than a minute he was unlocking her door and slipping inside the Forest Room, making his way with steely eyed determination to the bathing suite.

* * * * *

The sound of the door opening startled Kiley and she yelped, swinging around in the tub, covering her nakedness with the ineffectual span of her hands.

"What are you doing in here?" she squealed in a voice a full octave higher than her normal tone.

He didn't answer but came to the tub and bent over, scooping her up as though she weighed no more than a doll. Mindless of the water he sloshed onto his silk britches, of her wet body pressed against him, he carried her to the bed and laid her down, joining her in a lithe movement that would have done a panther proud.

Kiley made an attempt to elude him but he was up and over her, straddling her quivering body so she was trapped between his spread legs as he knelt on the bed, her hips touching his inner thighs. She tried to scoot up on the mattress but he fell forward, his elbows bracing him from crushing her with his weight.

"No," she said, but she heard the lack of conviction in her voice.

It had been a long time since she'd been with a man. Her body was aching with longing just looking up at this prime specimen of male flesh. She was already wet between the legs—which surprised the hell out of her—and the heaviness she felt there was a sure signal she needed to get laid. Her palms actually itched to touch his tanned skin. She wanted to wrap her arms around his shoulders and her legs around his hips and feel him sink deep into a body that had been too long without. *So wrong. It was so wrong to want this on so many levels.*

She didn't know this man but she'd never wanted a lover more than she did him. A part of her wanted to throw caution to the winds and take what he was offering. Another part—the prudent side of her nature—was screaming all sorts of warnings at her.

He stretched out atop her, wedging one leg between hers, pushing her thighs apart. Her wet flesh was sticking to his silk britches and the drag of it over her lower belly made her suck in her breath.

"Please don't," she whispered, putting her hands up to that broad, naked chest and reveling in the feel of the crisp wiriness beneath her fingers. Though she held him at bay, denying him what he so obviously wanted, she knew he would go no further than what she allowed. She shook her head. "Not like this."

His arms flexed on the mattress to either side of her shoulders as though he was asking why, letting her know his frustration.

"Let me talk to Mr. St. John," she said and watched him straighten, his arms now hanging loosely at his sides. When he moved, her hands slid down his chest to his taut belly. Reluctantly, she removed them. "I didn't come here for what you are offering but—"

He shook his head and was off the bed before she could finish. The removal of his hot body from hers made Kiley whimper with regret. It was that small sound that put the heat of his palm to the juncture of her thighs.

She didn't protest and she didn't push him away.

Kiley's body arched off the bed as he unerringly slid his middle finger deep between her nether lips. She reached up and grabbed the two lowest branches of the tree headboard and squeezed her eyes closed as that strong digit flexed upward and claimed her mysterious and glorious G-spot.

And—damn it—she was lost.

* * * * *

He smiled behind the mask as she clamped her legs tightly against his wrist. Her knees were bent, her feet pressing into the mattress as her sweet little bottom lifted from the bed to give him freer access. She was gripping the branches above her with fingers tightening and loosening, arching back and forth as though she was attempting to unscrew a lid from a jar. He stared hungrily at her lush breasts, flattened against her chest, and the coral tips that invited his mouth to taste. He promised himself before the night was through he would claim first one then the other and worry them until she screamed for mercy.

"Sean," he heard her sigh as he continued to work the inner nub of flesh that was just as hard as the erection straining his britches.

Her breasts looked so forlorn splayed to either side of her and he reached down with his free hand to rub his palms over one then the other in slow circles that had her panting, her flanks lifting higher off the bed. He palmed the nipples until they were like warm little pebbles then plucked at them with the tips of his fingers.

"Sean," she shouted as she squirmed on the bed, pulling against his hand as he rubbed at the depth of her passion.

* * * * *

Kiley could feel the itch in the very core of her and she knew when that tickle was relieved it would be a sensation unlike any she'd ever known. This man was playing her like an instrument of which he was a master and she could not have stopped him even had she wanted to. And, despite her earlier protests, clearly she didn't want him to stop.

Thrilling to his touch, aching with his ministrations, she was rushing toward an orgasm she knew would be soul shattering. When it came—reaching up to grasp her in hot fingers that drew her toward pure ecstasy—she screamed her release as wave after wave pulsed against his conquering fingers.

He thrust his fingers as far as they would go inside her as the walls of her vagina tightened around him. Her hips were clear of the bed, her back arched, the back of her head pressed deeply into her pillow. Finally, she shuddered and fell limp to the mattress, though her legs were still clamped tightly around his wrist.

She lay there—quivering from head to toe—feeling the aftermath of a release that brought the stars down from the heavens behind her tightly closed eyelids. She was panting, her heart racing. A dewy film of perspiration had formed on her upper lip and under the creases of her heavy breasts. She trembled one last time then opened her eyes to look up into the eyes of the man bent over her.

Those amber eyes were bright with possession. The man behind them knew he had pleasured her in a way she had never experienced before. His fingers were still inside her and he gently slid them out a little ways, but at her moan, he slid them in again, moving them within her before withdrawing them completely.

"Ummm," Kiley groaned. She smiled hesitantly at him, both intimidated and embarrassed by what had just happened.

For a moment he stood there looking down at her. He placed his fingertips to his mouth then laid them gently on Kiley's lips.

She could smell the muskiness of her own fluids on his fingers but it didn't matter to her. Normally, she would have been appalled by such an action, but she surprised herself when she pressed a kiss to those strong fingers.

The strength of his erection flexing against the wet fabric of his britches drew her attention and she drew in a slow breath. The bulge against the silk was huge and she knew the turgid flesh causing that bulge could pleasure her more than his knowing fingers. She was about to reach for him, to draw him to her when the phone rang.

Startled by the intrusion, her lover straightened, removing his fingers from her mouth. The sudden heat in his amber gaze told her he was more than annoyed by the interruption.

More disappointed than aggravated, Kiley bent over and grabbed the receiver from the small bedside table that looked like a gnarled stump.

"Hello?" she answered watching as the man in black leaned against the bedroom wall, his arms folded over his chest.

"Have you found him yet?" Greg Strickland asked.

"What?"

"Mr. Anchor Balls," Greg laughed. "I didn't hear from you yesterday. Did you land ho him today?"

Kiley's disappointment became aggravation at the inane patter. Her mouth tightened. "No, Greg, I haven't." She glanced up at the man in black and saw he was watching her intently. "I'm sure Dr. Carstairs will inform you when we're finished here."

There was a moment of silence then Greg's tone changed. "Is there someone there with you?"

"Yes."

"One of the infamous helpers?" came the snarled query.

"Yes."

Another moment of silence that lasted a beat or two longer. "You better tell me you've been photographing his cock, Kiley, and not having it jammed into you."

"Good night, Greg," Kiley said from between clenched teeth. "I'll tell Dr. Carstairs you called." Before Greg could say anything else, she hung up the phone.

The man in black had not moved. His amber eyes were locked on her face. There was something menacing about the way he was standing there. From his stance, she could almost feel the waves of anger that crashed toward her.

"Ah, that was my boss," she said. "The publisher of Dr. Carstairs's book. He wanted to know how things were going."

Without a word, her lover turned and walked out of the room.

Kiley frowned. What had just happened? It was almost as though he were jealous, but how could that be? He didn't know her and knew nothing of her relationship with Greg. Did he sense something in her tone as she talked to Greg that had sent alarm signals through his male ego?

"No," she said aloud, going back over the short conversation. There had been nothing in tone that would suggest she had known the man on the other end of the phone intimately. If anything, her tone had been rife with frustration and tinged with more than a little anger.

So what had caused Sean to pull another of his disappearance acts? And why would a gigolo care one way or the other if she did have a boyfriend? Most of the women that came here were married, for God's sake.

The whole incident needed to be forgotten. A finger-fuck orgasm with a silent brooding stalking man-whore was a one-off. Never to be repeated again. She needed to finish snapping photos of dicks and get home.

The sooner the better.

The clamminess of her body finally intruded Kiley's pondering and she realized she had never finished her bath. There was a fine film of soapsuds on her arms and legs, the feel of which was not conducive to a good night's sleep. Grimacing, she scooted off the bed and padded into the bathing suite. The water in the tub was tepid, scum-shot with grayish suds. Bending over, she turned off the jets of water, pulled the plug on the tub and entered the shower. She allowed the cooling bursts of water to calm her, but long after she had dried off and crawled naked between the satin sheets, she wondered why Sean's leaving still bothered her.

Chapter Seven

"Gregory Strickland," Henri reported to Julian the next morning, "is the owner of the Heartland Agency where Ms. Trevor is employed."

"How long have they been involved?"

Henri's left eyebrow quirked upward. "You never fail to amaze me, Julian. You have an uncanny ability to intuit things like this. I can't begin to understand how you do it," Henri said on a long sigh.

"Then don't try," Julian snapped. "How long?"

"Actually, they are not involved."

"But they were."

"For a short while," Henri replied. He glanced down at his notebook. "The affair started when they were working together on an assignment. The affair seems to be going nowhere. By all accounts, he's a prick and has it in everything that slows down long enough for him to poke. As far as can be determined, things are at an impasse between them."

"An impasse I intend to put to an end," Julian stated.

Henri closed his notebook. "Do I detect interest here, Julian?" he asked, a worried frown etched between his brows. "Have you allowed yourself to become attracted to this young woman?"

"What if I have?"

Clicking the point of his ever-present pen, Henri put the instrument in his inside coat pocket. "Is that wise, my friend?" he inquired. "All things considered?"

"I'm no longer a child, Henri," Julian said but his words were soft, spoken with affection. "I know what I'm doing."

"I hope so, Julian," Henri replied. "For all our sakes, I sincerely hope so."

* * * * *

The helper with the flaming-red pubic hair was the twelfth penis to be inspected since she'd started. The young man's nether head had been as red and angry as the stormy expression in his dark green eyes. His stance made it clear to Kiley that he resented having his genitalia inspected by the constant flexing of his thigh muscles, the annoyed snorts and clucking of his tongue.

Kiley had to bite her lower lip to keep from laughing. When she took the last photo—not having found the telltale anchor-shaped birthmark on this young man—she looked up, drawing his eyes to hers.

"You are a very well-equipped young man," she said and watched as a ripple of pride sparked through his stare. "I can certainly understand why the ladies all ask for Big Red."

Those green eyes turned a few shades darker and the stiff posture that had held the young man at a distance relaxed. He ducked his head and—would wonders never cease—actually dug a childish toe into the sand, wobbling his muscular leg from side to side. Had he been able to speak, Kiley was sure he'd have said, "Aw, shucks, ma'am, it ain't *that* big."

"Thank you," Kiley said softly. "Your contribution to Dr. Carstairs's book will certainly draw many a jealous eye."

Once more that toe dug into the sand then the young man lifted his head. Kiley could feel the smile behind the silken mask. He seemed almost reluctant to leave and she had the impression he wanted to hear more compliments on his well-endowed manhood.

Number thirteen was lurking at the edge of the water and as soon as his predecessor left he came ambling over. As naked as the day he was born, as powerfully built as any Mr. Universe, his bulging muscles rippled in the sun, the well-oiled flesh gleaming as he came to plant himself before her. Hands on hips, he bent his masked head and locked eyes with her.

Kiley said hello and smiled pleasantly. She looked down at his small offering and almost groaned. As big as the man was, his miniscule penis was surely a disappointment to him. The fact that he was uncircumcised—the first she had encountered—made her curious. Without thinking, she reached out and took the little member in her hand and before she could draw a breath, it expanded. She snatched her hand back but she heard his low chuckle and looked up.

Her face burning brightly, she was made even more uncomfortable by the knowing look in his pale gray eyes.

"A woman gains more pleasure from an uncut penis than one that has had the foreskin removed," Dr. Carstairs had said. *"You should try Derek while you're at the Cay and you'll see what I mean."*

"Derek?" Kiley muttered.

The young man nodded and that knowing look turned hot. He was standing there, arms akimbo, straight-as-an-arrow cock pointed right at Kiley. What she had thought was a little penis was now a shaft of considerable length and breadth.

"Stand to the side, please," Kiley managed to ask as she hastily snatched up her camera. She took shots of his left profile and shots of his right, straight on, and then asked him to lift his penis upward.

He obliged but as he did, he moved his hand back and forth slowly, manipulating it with a seductive ease that turned Kiley's blush fiery red.

"Ah, t-that's all I need," she mumbled. No anchor birthmark on that small scrotum but what a prow he had.

"Are you sure?" he whispered from behind the mask.

Shocked that he would speak to her, she had to swallow past the lump in her throat. She bobbed her head eagerly. "Yes, thank you."

He shrugged and turned to go, his stiff erection like a battering ram thrust straight out in front of him.

"Oh my," Kiley said, fanning her blazing face. She set down the camera and reached for a bottle of iced water in the cooler beside her. As she did, she saw Sean standing about ten feet behind her.

He was clad in a pair of very skimpy swim briefs, his perfectly tanned body looking far more delicious than any man's had a right to look. Standing with his legs apart, arms crossed over his chest, he was an invitation she wished she could openly accept.

"I haven't photographed you," she heard herself saying.

Sean made no move toward her. Instead he looked to his left and when Kiley followed his stare was disappointed that another helper was trudging his way toward her through the hot sand.

"You are next, okay?" she asked.

A careless shrug was his answer.

The fourteenth penis, she thought as the young black man presented himself to her. She smiled and asked her subject to remove his skin-tight white shorts.

This one took great delight in peeling off his shorts and did so as though he was listening to music to strip by. Slow and deliberate, teasing, he dipped the shorts first in the back, then the front, then wiggled them down his hips, shaking his hips from side to side as the shorts moved farther south.

And those slim hips weren't the only things moving side to side.

Kiley gulped as his huge member—heavily veined and as dark as rich chocolate—swung between his taut thighs. She was shocked that he had no pubic hair at all and that his lower belly looked as smooth as a baby's bottom. There didn't appear to be any hair on his slick body. When that large penis became a rotary tool, making a full 360-degree arc as his hips undulated and he swung it without the aid of his hands, her mouth dropped open.

She could hear Sean laughing as she sat there hypnotized by the performance of Mr. Fourteen and she wasn't altogether sure that wasn't an appropriate measurement of the weapon he was wielding with such merry abandon. She could not keep her head from following the rotation of that happy cock.

"Ah, I need to take pictures of that," Kiley said a bit too loudly and heard Sean's snort of derision. Not daring to look at her tormentor, she pleaded silently with the young man showing off in front of her to behave.

When she was finished with the pictures, she turned around to motion Sean over but he was gone.

"Oh, shit," she exploded, stomping her foot in the sand. Once more, he had pulled his disappearing act and she was more annoyed than ever.

There were no more helpers headed toward her although the beach was full of them. Off to her right was a naked volleyball game that held a dozen or so women in complete thrall.

Having enough for one day, Kiley gathered her camera and the beach tote she had brought along and headed for the cabana where liquor was being served. She needed something cold and potent to help assuage both the irritation and disappointment she was feeling.

* * * * *

Julian watched her from his office as she straddled one of the bamboo stools and ordered a drink. He could sense the frustration building in her and made a mental wager that it wouldn't be too long before she came to seek him out.

"You've changed your mind about participating, haven't you, sweetness?" he asked. "And you're going to ask for Sean, aren't you? I wonder what your fantasy will be."

He gave her half an hour to build up her courage, so while that was happening, he went to shower. Stepping out of the black swim briefs, he stood under the water with his face turned into the spray, his hands braced to either side of the wall in front of him. Lowering his head, he let the water beat down on his shoulders, relaxing him. As he toweled dry, he ignored the building erection that came of its own accord whenever he thought of Kiley Trevor.

"It won't be long, old friend," he whispered, drawing the rough towel over his sensitive flesh.

Six months, he thought as he dressed in black jeans and tank top. It had been six months since he'd allowed a woman to touch him.

The phone on his desk was ringing as he left his dressing room. He snatched it up. "What?" he snapped.

"I have that call ready for you," Henri said, seemingly unperturbed by the harsh greeting. "Is now a good time?"

Julian felt his blood begin to pound in the column of his neck. "Yes," he said, almost choking on the word.

"Do you have a pen? I'll give you the number."

Grabbing a pen, Julian mumbled his readiness.

"It's area code 563…" Henri began then gave Julian the rest of the number; he said it was unlisted.

"Ms. Trevor will be on her way up to see me in—" Julian glanced at the gold Rolex watch on his right wrist "—about ten minutes. Would you waylay her for me until five o'clock then send her up?"

"Of course," Henri agreed and ended the call.

For a moment or two Julian stood there with his hand on the phone's cradle. His heart was racing and he could feel perspiration dripping between his breastbones. He took a deep breath then began dialing.

He didn't expect anyone to answer. When the sweet voice on the other end said hello, he froze for a moment, unable to speak.

"Is there someone there?"

"Do you…" Julian asked, closing his eyes. He swallowed. "Do you remember the words to the Connemara Cradle Song?"

He heard a quick intake of breath and felt the blood pounding in his temples. When the next word came, he felt his knees buckle and reached out to grab the chair.

"Patrick?" It was said so softly, so hopefully. "Patrick, is that you?"

"Do you remember the words?" he repeated.

"I could never forget the songs I sang to you, Paddy."

He could hear tears in the voice as the woman on the other end began singing, the melody the same as the old folk tune "Down in the Valley."

"'On the wings of the wind, o'er the dark rolling deep...'"

The voice broke and he could hear sobs and a low male voice saying soothing words.

"'Angels are coming to watch o'er thy sleep'," Julian finished and felt tears sliding down his cheeks.

"How could you remember that?" she asked. "You were just a baby."

"Even babies know when they are loved," he replied and reached up to swipe at the tears scalding him. "I remember being loved."

"I didn't give you up, Paddy," she said forcefully. "I would never have given you up if I had had a choice."

"I know," he said, biting his trembling lip.

"Were they...did they...?" she couldn't seem to finish.

A man's voice came over the line. "She's just crying, son. She's okay."

"Is this Mr. Lynden?" Julian asked, stiffening at the sound of the voice.

"Call me Bradford," the man replied. "I'm your mother's husband."

"I need to talk with her, Bradford. I—"

"Give her awhile to adjust to this, son. Call her back tomorrow," he said then his voice was muffled as he covered the phone. Though his words were unclear, his tone was stern before he came back on the line. "I'm going to calm her down before we go any further with this. She has high blood pressure and I don't want her getting worked up any more than she already is. She's spent all these years trying to find you. A few hours won't make any difference."

"You sure she's all right?"

"Yes and now that's she's found you again, she'll be better yet."

"She knows where I am. She knows what I am," Julian said and shame shuddered through him. "The detective she sent..."

"That doesn't matter to her. She just wants to see her son," Bradford said.

After Julian hung up, promising to call back in the next day, he paced the confines of his office, thrusting his hand repeatedly through his hair. He had forgotten all about Kiley Trevor's visit and when the knock came at his door, he flung it open, knowing his face showed signs of fury at the interruption.

Kiley stepped back from the look on his face. He was glaring at her, his breath coming in ragged gasps.

"I'm s-sorry," she stammered. "Obviously, I've come at the wrong time."

"No," he said and reached for her, dragging her into his office and slamming the door behind her.

Kiley started around him. "I'll come back later."

He blocked her exit. "You wanted to ask me to send Sean to you," he said and his eyes flared.

Kiley opened her mouth. *She better not say no, he growled inside his head.* She merely nodded.

"What fantasy?" he snapped.

She blinked. "Excuse me?"

He threw out his hand. "To have a helper assigned to you, you need a fantasy."

Clearly, she was at a loss for words and completely stymied by the statement. She shrugged helplessly. "I don't—"

"Pirate? Medieval knight? Indian warrior? Construction worker?" he rattled off. "You name it, lady, and Sean will be it."

She stood there mute, as if she was ticking off the options in her head.

"A cowboy," Julian grated, his teeth clenched. "You like cowboys?"

"Ah, yes, but—"

"Then go back to your room and I'll send him to you later this evening."

"Well, I don't know, I—"

He didn't allow her to finish. He took her arm and showed her to the door, opening it for her and practically shoving her into the corridor. "He'll be there," he snarled. "He needs you as much as you need him."

With that, he shut the door in her face.

Chapter Eight

He was dressed like a cowboy who had just ridden into town looking for trouble. The black cotton shirt—slightly soiled with what looked like trail dust—was open halfway down his tanned chest. The black leather gun belt slung low over his lean hips and tied to one muscular thigh held a lethal-looking Colt Peacemaker with a pearl handle. Around his neck was a black bandana tied in a careless knot at the side of his throat. Black leather gloves, dusty black boots with slightly tarnished spurs, and a black Stetson with a silver concho headband completed the picture of a gunslinger on the prowl. Over his shoulder was draped a pair of worn leather saddlebags.

"Evening, ma'am," he said in a thick southern drawl as he touched the tip of his left index finger to his hat in greeting.

Kiley swallowed and clutched the silken robe she wore closer to her throat. His deep voice sent shivers down her spine. The tone was just above a seductive whisper and had surprised her before she remembered Julian St. John telling her the only way a helper could talk to a guest was during a fantasy. Hearing Sean speak sent flutters through her lower belly. Her eyes drank him in like a woman dying of thirst before whom a tall, cold glass of water had been placed.

Gone was the full-face mask. It had been replaced by the kind of mask like the one worn by the Lone Ranger. Beneath the Stetson was silky black hair that curled low on his neck. Behind the eyeholes, those amber orbs were smoldering.

She watched, unable to move as he shrugged away the saddlebags, letting them drop to the chair beside the door. Her heart began to pound as he took off his hat and laid it atop the saddlebags.

"I've come a long way to find you, Sara," he said in a low voice and his hands went to the buckle of the gun belt.

Kiley took a step backward, dragging in shallow breaths as she watched him remove the gun belt.

"If he wants to fight for you, I'm willing."

She thrilled to his words, beginning to shiver as he laid the gun belt aside and began pulling the tail of his shirt from his gabardine britches.

She took another step back, then another as he began unbuttoning the cuffs of his long-sleeve black shirt. His eyes were locked on hers.

"I'll kill any man who thinks he can take you away from me."

Her knees were weak as those words sank into her feverish mind. His hands were on the front of his shirt, working the buttons until the dark fabric hung open. Then the belt circling his britches was unhooked and drawn slowly from the loops.

"Oh, lord," Kiley muttered, taking another step away from the purposeful glint in those golden eyes. She glanced down at her bare feet and instinctively put one atop the other like a little girl.

"Come here," he said, unfastening the button at the top of his britches, "and I'll make you forget he ever existed."

She shook her head, backing away from him, suddenly leery of this tall, dangerous man with the low, commanding voice. When her back met the wall behind her, her eyes flared. She would have darted away but he was on her quicker than she could move, his body pressed to hers. Before she could push him away, he had her wrists in his hands and was lifting her arms, anchoring her hands to either side of her head, leaning into her.

"Do you want me to get rid of him?" he asked.

Kiley could feel his hot breath against her cheek as he pushed his lower body against hers. The hard bulge of his erection made her groan.

"Do you want me to fight him?"

"Who?" she managed to whisper, lost in the headiness of his nearness.

"If he touches you again, I'll slit his worthless throat," Sean said in a menacing tone.

She felt his lips on the side of her neck and gave herself up to the glorious feel of his tongue dragging across the span of her throat, delving into the hollow where her erratic heartbeat pulsed, then he flicked at the underside of her chin.

His right hand slid slowly down her upraised arm until his palm was flattened over her silk-clad breast. His fingers gently cupped her, his thumb grazing the bud that leapt to life at the touch.

"I have searched for you all my life," he said, his voice thick with emotion. "I won't ever let you go. Don't even try to leave me, Sara."

She opened her mouth to protest but he slanted his lips across hers and his tongue thrust possessively inside. The very force of the kiss threatened to sweep her legs out from under her. She sagged against the wall, sucking in a harsh breath through her nose when he shoved his leg between hers and braced her body on his hard thigh. The heat of his flesh through the rough gabardine, the rigidity of his limb pushing against her throbbing core, the press of his chest to her united to mold her to him as though they were one entity.

"Love me," he whispered hoarsely, his lips dragging from her mouth to her cheek. "I need you to love me."

Was her mind playing tricks or was he that good an actor, because she would swear she heard immense need in Sean's words. His voice was filled with a longing she responded to deep in her soul. She had felt his hunger in the passionate press of his lips upon hers. She had tasted it on his tongue, upon the fullness of his full lips.

"This isn't a fantasy, Sara," he said. "For me, this is real. I have wanted you from the first day I saw you step off the ship."

"You were watching me?" she asked.

"I was devouring you, sweet Sara," he whispered, his lips at her ear. He flicked his tongue along the silky spiral and she shivered. His warm breath was invading her body, sending clenches of lust through her belly. "I became lost in your beauty and I knew I had to have you." His palm gently squeezed and he molded her beneath her robe, pushing upward lightly. "I vowed I'd make you mine and there would never be another man to lay hands to you."

His words were sending chills of pleasure rippling up and down her spine. He might have been playacting, carrying on a scenario he had performed countless times with other women, but her investigator instincts told her that was not the case. She heard sadness beneath his words. She heard loneliness being dredged up from the man's very soul.

"We were made to be together, Sara," he said, his kisses trailing from her ear down the side of her neck and onto her shoulder. His thumb was sweeping across her erect nipple and sending shudders of delight down her side. "We were destined to be together."

Her hands were splayed across his powerful chest and she could feel his heart thundering. If what he was doing was nothing more than an act—a routine he had perfected over the years—his blood would not be rushing so quickly through his veins, she reasoned. He would be blasé about the whole thing, calm, methodical and not quivering beneath her hands when she leaned into him.

"I need you, Sara," he whispered and claimed her mouth once more. His kiss was long, hard, and draining, and when his lips slid from hers, he gathered her to him, his arms going around her to crush her tightly to him.

In for a penny, in for a pound. If it's an act, he'll think she's playing along. If not, maybe he'll know her words were true. "I need you, too, Sean," she replied. "I have needed you all my life."

He ran his hands beneath her hips, lifted her up. She threw her arms around his neck and wrapped her legs around his lean hips. As he turned and started for the bedroom, she could feel the leap of his cock probing at her rump with each step he took.

The bedroom suite was dark but he knew where to find the bed. Once he was there, he bent forward, allowing her to fall away from his taut body. Reluctantly, she let go of her hold on his neck, unwrapped her legs from his waist as she felt the depression of the mattress against her back. Without a word, she dug her heels into the coverlet and scooted backwards, giving him room to join her there on the edge, but Sean was undoing his britches, flicking the buttons aside with haste. When the last button was opened, he sat down beside her and began pulling off his boots.

"You want me to take you like that, sweet Sara?" he asked, one corner of his mouth lifted in challenge. "Or are you gonna take off that robe?" Before she could answer, he tossed aside his boot and looked around at her. "Or would you like me to rip it off you?"

"No!" she said, liking the garment too much to see it destroyed. She came to her knees on the bed and stripped out of the robe.

She heard him draw in a breath as his gaze fell to her breasts. He gave a slight little smile. "I'll damned sure have you screaming this time," he said enigmatically.

"Screaming?" she said, blinking.

"In a good way, sweet Sara," he promised. "Screaming with pleasure, ma'am."

His back was to her as he peeled off his socks. She reached out to draw her hands along his naked shoulders, down the strong column of his spine as he leaned back to pull away his britches. She put her arms around him as he kicked free of the gabardine, running the palms of her hands over his shoulders and onto the flexing muscles of his pecs.

Sean laid his head back, giving her access to slide her lips on the side of his neck. He smiled, his breath coming in a quicker, much shallower cadence. While her hands roamed freely over his chest, her fingers stroking his nipples to stiff little pebbles, he reached behind him to rest his hands on her hips.

"Tell me," she said, her lips against his ear, "what you want, cowboy."

"You," he said with a grunt.

She rubbed against him. "For how long? An hour? The night?"

His arms entrapped her, jerking her to him as he plastered his hands on her rump, digging his fingers into her flesh.

"For the rest of my life," he growled.

"You mean for as long as the fantasy lasts," she said and heard the bitterness in her voice.

He moved so quickly, she could not stop the yelp of surprise that squeaked from her throat. One moment she was behind him, the next she was sprawled on her back, her legs splayed wide and his heavy body lying atop her.

"Let's get one thing straight," he said, looming over her, taking her wrists in his strong hands and holding them to the mattress. "I always swore that when I found the right woman, when I staked claim to her, I would never let her go."

His words sent a chill down her spine but excited her at the same time. This man was issuing a challenge and though his face was in shadow, she could feel the hot glare in his golden eyes.

"Do you think Julian St. John will allow you to do that?" she asked, holding her breath for the answer.

"Do you want me?" he countered and she knew the words had been spoken from between clenched teeth.

She let go of the restraint she'd always held on her wayward heart. "Yes, I do," she answered honestly.

For the space of a few heartbeats he said nothing but let go of her wrists then stretched out so that his head was on her shoulder, his lean body now half atop hers, his heavy weight shifted so she would be more comfortable.

She gathered him to her, threading her fingers through his thick hair below the mask. His free hand was pressed palm down between her breasts, one long leg arced across hers.

"All my life," he said so softly she had to strain to hear his words, "I have wanted what normal men take for granted—a home, a wife, maybe children one day. I've always wanted the white picket fence and the draping wisteria. I'd trade my Porsche in for a SUV in a heartbeat."

Kiley smiled. "Okay, then, I'll trade you," she chuckled.

He traced a lazy figure eight on her chest and belly, circling her belly button and coming upward again.

"I grew up hating wealth," he continued. "I despised dressing for supper. I detested prim and proper school uniforms that required precision-tied tie knots and shoes so shiny you could see your face in them."

"I grew up envying wealth," she told him. "I despised using toilet paper instead of napkins during our meals. I detested wearing dresses that had been handed down from my cousins and trying to cram my feet into shoes I'd outgrown the year before."

"I have more money than I'll ever be able to spend."

"I may have to declare bankruptcy when I get back to Iowa," she sighed.

"I killed a man."

"I—" Kiley stopped, her lips parting in shock. "What did you say?"

"I can't ever leave Mistral Cay."

Because he had been speaking so softly, almost whispering his confessions to her, she had not noticed the southern drawl had fled his voice. It wasn't until he told her he could not leave the resort that she fully realized who it was that was lying beside her.

He seemed to be waiting for her to respond to his words. She could hear his quick, expectant breath and pictured the mysterious, commanding Julian St. John in her mind's eye. It might be hard for her to accept that a man as sensuous as Sean could kill someone but she had no such uncertainties where Julian was concerned. His was a domineering personality for which she did not care.

"Whom did you kill, Julian?" she finally asked.

"That doesn't matter."

She searched the shadows overhead, tracing the branches of the headboard arched above them. There were secrets in her life she certainly didn't want people to know but at least she'd committed no crimes that were punishable by death in most countries.

"Where was this?" she questioned.

"In the States," he said.

"In a state with a death penalty?"

"Yes," he answered.

Pain drove through her heart. No, she thought, as her arms tightened around him, he could never leave the Cay. To do so would be unthinkable.

"Was it premeditated?"

"It was self-defense, but I couldn't prove it."

She thought about that for a long time, allowing the silence to spin around them, enveloping them in a cocoon of shared knowledge.

"Does the law know where you are?" she asked.

"My worst enemy does and in the past he's hired men to try to take me off the Cay. He'd like nothing better than to see me in prison awaiting execution. So far, I've managed to stay a few steps ahead of him. There hasn't been a new helper at the resort in five years and I don't allow any ships except my own yacht to dock here."

She felt him removing the mask and could not resist running her fingers over his face. The hair at his temples was damp and she smoothed it back from his forehead.

"Aren't you afraid I might turn you in?" she queried.

"I don't think so."

"Why not?"

"Not your style, sweetness," he said with a snort.

"And just what is my style?" she countered, tilting her head. "Should I call you Sean or Julian?"

"Call me whatever you like," he answered. "Do you want me to go on calling you Sara?"

She tensed. "What do you mean?"

"Your real name is Kiley Trevor and you work for the Heartland Detective Agency," he replied. "A few months ago you had an affair with your boss Greg Strickland but realized the man's nothing more than a walking cumstick."

Stunned that he knew her true identity, Kiley was taken aback. She remained silent as he recited the particulars of her life from where she was born to where she bought cat food for her beloved Xander.

"You know why I'm here," she said, staring into his handsome face.

"You're looking for Patrick O'Reilly, Fay Lynden's son," he stated.

She groaned. "And I bet you know which one of the helpers he is, don't you?"

"Yes."

"And have been keeping him away from me while I…" She could feel the heat turning on in her cheeks. "You bastard," she griped, punching his shoulder.

He laughed and slid his arm over her, his fingers tucked beneath her rib cage. "Weren't you having fun?" he asked.

"Oh, loads of it," she mumbled. "Nothing like comparing cucumbers to zucchinis."

"With a bean sprout every now and then to break the monotony?" he joked.

"You were enjoying my discomfort," she accused.

"Tremendously," he admitted. "That's why I went down to the beach to watch. You seemed—ah—totally preoccupied with your task."

She giggled and cuddled closer to him. "You are a true cad, Julian St. John."

"I only provided what you asked for, ma'am," he said with a chuckle.

"Well, it was a hot, hands-on job but someone had to do it," she stated. "I notice you never volunteered to show me your dangly."

"Wanna see it now?" he asked with an arched brow.

"I'm sure I'll have the opportunity to get up close and personal with it at some time," she said with a titter. "Why didn't you just tell me you were Julian?"

"Would you have called me to you if you had known who I really was?" he countered.

Kiley blushed. "No," she replied honestly. "Julian St. John is an intimidating man."

"But Sean isn't," he stated.

"Sean is sexy as hell and every woman's dream," she replied. "I think a waiter once told me that."

"A waiter whose mouth I should have washed out," he said with a grunt.

"You set about to seduce me," she said. "From that first day?"

"From the moment I saw you," he said.

"I still have a job to do here," she said. "I—"

"Stay with me," he asked. All the humor had fled his tone.

"I can't," she said. "I was paid to do a job and I intend to see it through."

He thought about that for a moment. "All right. But when it's over, you will stay here with me."

"I'll need to go back and get my things. I—"

"I can send Henri and Christian to do that," he cut her off.

"No," she said. "There are things I have to do and—"

"He could grab you," he said. "My enemy has spies here I haven't been able to ferret out and by now I'm sure he knows how I feel about you."

"How would he know?" she asked. "Hell, I don't even know."

"I don't use the persona of Sean often. When I do, it's never with one of our clients. The mole would have reported it to my enemy by now."

"All right," she said. "But why would you need to pretend to be Sean if—"

"There is an old friend," he interrupted. "An acquaintance who comes a few times each year. I use that persona with her."

Jealousy rippled through Kiley's breast. "Who is she?"

"Celeste Dubois," he answered.

Kiley's eyebrows shot up. "The ex-nun turned madam?"

"That's a stupid rumor started by a rival," Julian said with a snort. "Celeste is Romanian, a gypsy. She came to the U.S. when she was nineteen. By the time she was twenty-one, she was being heralded as the most versatile lady of the night to be found in the French Quarter. If there is an act of love in which Celeste is not a master, it does not merit learning."

"I'm so impressed," Kiley mumbled, drawing the second word out disdainfully.

Julian laughed. "You should be. You will reap the benefits of her expertise in the art of love. Celeste only tutors those she feels are worthy of her attention and she has taught me everything she knows."

"La-de-da," she quipped, rolling her eyes. "Ain't I a lucky little girl?"

"Would you like to find out just how lucky?" he muttered, his lips pressed once more to her throat.

"Why does she come here?" Kiley demanded. "Doesn't she have a stable of boy toys to play with in New Orleans?"

"I was one of her boy toys," Julian said quietly. "I owe her."

Kiley's gaze turned hard. "So you have to repay her by servicing her for the rest of your life?"

"No," he said. "I'm sure when she finds out about you and me, that part of our relationship will cease."

"You think so?" she asked and hated the nasty tone in her voice. Jealousy was something she hadn't experienced since high school. Not even Greg's numerous peccadilloes had caused her a moment's concern, but just thinking of Sean—she disliked the name Julian—in the arms of a high-priced courtesan brought out the green-eyed monster in her.

"She brought me here, sweetness," Julian said, obviously preferring that name to Kiley since the way he said it sent shivers down her spine. "She set me up in business. Our arrangement has been mutually beneficial."

"Does she know about the man you killed?"

"She knows. Without her help, I would have been caught long ago."

"And so she holds it over your head and you jump whenever she tells you, huh?"

She felt him wince. "That's not the way it is. You're trying to paint her as a villainess and she isn't."

For a moment they were both quiet. He had threaded his fingers with hers. When she finally broke the silence, she heard his breathing cease and knew he was anticipating rejection.

"It doesn't matter," she said. "The next time she comes here, I'll have a little talk with her. The sooner she knows I intend to fight for you, the—"

"Fight for *me*?" he asked. There was incredulity in his tone.

"I've never really had anything in life that I ever truly wanted," she said. "I've lived in poverty—one step ahead of the collection agencies—all my life. I lost count of the times we had our electricity turned off. You'd think I would have learned from my parents' mistakes but I didn't. My credit is piss-poor, but I'm trying to build it up before I wind up having to file bankruptcy. I've never had a real home and I've never had a man who loved me for who I am."

"I think that's where we're heading, don't you?" he asked gently.

"Maybe," she answered. "Being unable to keep our hands off one another is a step in the right direction, I guess. I really don't know. I've never loved anyone before."

"Neither have I," he admitted.

"I'm a logical woman," she said. "I'm a down-to-earth woman. I don't make decisions lightly—especially not ones that will affect the rest of my life. I've got to think about all this."

"What is there to think about?" he asked, and she could hear the fear of rejection rampant in his sexy voice.

"I have to think about what I want and what I need," she replied. "What is right for you and for me."

"I want you," he said. "I need you. I don't know anything I can say to help you make the decision to stay with me."

"We really don't know that much about one another, though," she protested. "We—"

"I know I want to lay the world at your feet, sweetness. I want to give you everything you've ever wanted. I don't want you to ever lack for anything."

"You don't think that smacks of buying a woman's love?" she countered.

"*Could* I buy your love?" he asked.

She shook her head. "Never. It's not for sale."

"Neither is mine," he told her. "I used to think there was no such thing as love at first sight but then I'd never seen you before. The moment I did, something twisted inside me and I knew I'd move heaven and earth to make you mine."

Chapter Nine

He was laying himself bare to her. He was revealing things that gave her an immense hold over him. His admission of having killed a man wasn't as horrifying to her as she suspected he thought it was. In her line of work, she'd seen men killed—had shot a few herself, though she'd never taken a life. If Sean had killed a man in self-defense—as he had claimed it to be—she could understand why he had fled the States, especially if his enemy was a powerful man intent on destroying him.

"What are you thinking, sweetness?" he asked, his eyes filled with trepidation.

"I want you," she said and with that took her hand out of his. She slid her palm down his chest and cupped his cock. "I want this."

"Kiley—"

"Hush," she said. "No more talking, cowboy." She massaged his length and smiled as it leapt in her hand. "Let's seal this deal now. We can go over the particulars later."

He had no chance to protest; she moved away from him to kneel on the bed. As she flung one leg over his hip and pushed him flat on his back, she leaned back to sit on his knees.

"Am I hurting you?" she asked, both hands on his erection now.

"No," he said in a ragged whisper.

"You're sure?"

"Yes."

"Wait a minute," she said and was off the bed before he could stop her.

"Get your ass back here, woman," he shouted. She watched him prop himself up on his elbows as she disappeared into the bathroom.

"Don't get your long johns in a bunch, cowboy," she called out.

She came back and hopped up on the tall mattress. Straddling him once more, she put her hand on his chest to urge him down once more.

"Sweetness, I—"

"If you don't shut up, I'm gonna gag you," she said sternly.

He snorted.

"Let's see if I remember how to do this," she said.

"Do what?" he asked, frowning, for there was a squishing sound that made him lift his head from the pillow. "Sweetness? What are you doing?"

She reached for him, taking his now flaccid cock in hands that were slick with hand cream. What was limp one second leapt to life in the next and she heard him sigh.

Smoothing the cream over the entire expanse of his hard cock, Kiley slid the lightly cupped fingers of her right hand down the length of him, twisting gently, while she polished the head of his penis with the palm of her left hand.

Julian reached up behind him to grab the lowest hanging branch of the headboard. His breath rate had increased and his thighs beneath her were almost rigid.

While holding his cock against his belly, she gently scratched her fingernails from the underside of his shaft, down his balls then turned her hand so she could slide her middle finger all the way to his anus.

"Shit," Julian gasped.

"You'd better not," she warned, inserting the tip of her middle fingernail into the puckered opening.

He grabbed for her but she swatted his hands away.

"No," she said. "You are mine to do with as I please, cowboy. Now behave."

He was at her mercy and seemed to resign himself to the delicious torment as she dragged her fingernails up his scrotum, flicking the taut ridges of his scrotal sac. Palming his rigid cock between her hands, she rubbed downward, alternating in a back and forth motion then upward again, the slickness of the cream causing little friction but the desired effect, which had him panting. While wrapping the fingers of her left hand around the shaft, she removed her middle finger from his puckered hole then delicately touched the fingernail of her index finger into the slit.

He groaned and she could feel his body quivering.

"My, my," she said in a husky voice. "You are leaking like a sieve, cowboy!"

His juices were mixing with the cream on her hands, adding more lubrication to her ministrations.

Cupping his balls in the palm of her right hand, she rolled them gently, ignoring his moans as she turned her attention to the seminal vesicles on the sides of his sac, using her thumb and middle finger to stroke them first in tandem then in opposing movement.

"Kiley," he warned in a low growl that seemed to come from the depths of his chest.

She rose up on one knee and used the other to push his legs apart. When she was sitting between his spread thighs, she ordered him to put his feet on her shoulders.

"What?" he asked, lifting his head to look at her through the darkness.

"Do as you're told, cowboy," she demanded. "And no backtalk, mister."

He hesitated for a second or two then braced his ankles over her shoulders.

"Men have a G-spot, too," she said. "Did you know that?"

He didn't get a chance to answer. She leaned forward, bending his knees toward his chest. His ass was off the mattress, arched toward her, as exposed as a man could be. Her right thumb moved under that super-sensitive area between the base of his scrotum and anus. She stroked, searching for the dimple, and when she found it, pressed it softly for the count of ten then relaxed the pressure before applying it again.

Julian arched his hips up as though he had been struck by lightning. He was groaning, the sounds coming out with each expulsion of breath. His gasps were loud, his reaction instant when her middle finger slipped into his anus and wiggled playfully.

"Damn!" he shrilled. "I can't... I'm going to..."

As her finger probed deeper into his anal opening, she used her other hand to grip the head of his shaft and begin rotating it from side to side as though she were turning a faucet on and off, pulling the shaft upward as she manipulated him.

He came as explosively as any man she had ever been with. The hot spurt of his cum hit her palm and ran down her wrist. She groaned in satisfaction and, when he shuddered one final time, she reached for the towel she had brought from the bathroom. While he lay twitching from the aftermath of his orgasm, she gently cleaned him, wiping the residual juices from his flesh and hers.

"When was the last time you got laid, cowboy?" she asked.

"Months," he whispered.

"I can believe it," she said. "You were chock-full, baby."

She would have thought he would fall asleep—for that had been her experience that sated men in the past. She was content to allow him to rest for she instinctively knew that when he turned his full attention to satisfying her, she would be fulfilled as she never had been. Stretching out beside him, placing her hand on his still-heaving chest, she had resigned herself to wait.

But, apparently, waiting was the last thing on Julian St. John's mind.

And surprise was the name of the game.

Stunned when he sat up and clapped his hands, she had no time to wonder what he was about for the branches above her came to twinkling life as tiny lights blinked on in random patterns through the silken leaves.

"Oh," Kiley breathed, staring up into what looked like fireflies flitting through the carved branches. She was mesmerized by the display, following the movement with her eyes as first one light then two then three flickered to catch her attention. There was just enough light from the branches for her to see his handsome face peering down at her. His dark hair glistened beneath the shimmer of the lights in the branches.

"All my life," he said, "I have wanted a woman who wanted my pleasure as much as her own."

"Then lie beside me and let me hold you," she said softly.

"No," he countered. "Now it's my turn."

As the imitation fireflies blinked through the leaves above her, Kiley discovered what true sexual expertise could be. Begrudgingly she thanked Celeste Dubois.

His hands were like rough silk as they dragged over her tender flesh. He stroked here, probed there, flicked in another spot. His palms soothed over her belly, cupped her breasts and his thumbs brought her nipples to hard little pebbles. His fingers threaded through her hair, massaged her scalp. His short fingernails grazed her belly button and gently spiraled down into the shallow indention, tickling the sensitive folds. He used the backs of his hands to trace the flesh on her rib cage and hips and down her thighs. He centered the palm of his right hand against the heat at the juncture of her thighs and held it there as she wiggled against him.

The heat from his hand was scalding her, bringing her juices, causing a deep stirring in her belly. Just as he had done, she reached up behind her and wrapped her fingers around the lowest branch.

"Open your legs," he whispered.

Like a raw recruit jumping at the command of her drill instructor, she jerked her legs apart, reveling in the feeling, for his hand was still pressed tightly to her.

The moment his middle finger slid into her, she arched her head back and squeezed her eyes shut. Deprived of seeing his handsome face, she immersed herself in the sensation his finger was creating between her folds. That strong length had gone unerringly to her G-spot and was rubbing it gently.

"Imagine my cock inside you," he said, using his free hand to pluck at the nipple of her right breast. "Imagine it deep inside you. Hard as a piece of smooth iron, warm as liquid fire."

Kiley moaned, lifting her hips toward his conquering hand.

"Can you feel the hot semen oozing into your core?"

She bit her lower lip, nodding as best she could with her head thrown back.

He jerked his finger inside her. "Do you feel the life in that stiff cock?"

"Umm," she groaned and flicked her tongue over her upper lip.

"He wants to go deeper into you. He wants to reach the very center of your pleasure."

He circled her G-spot with the pad of his fingertip then eased out of her to rub her clit.

"Outside?" he said, fingering her clitoris, "or inside?" Once more, his finger found the blazing sensitivity on the roof of her vagina. "Outside? Inside?"

He was turning her into a boneless mass of quivering flesh. She was panting, moaning, shuddering as he alternated the areas of his attention.

Then he lowered his lips to her breast and drew the nipple into his mouth, capturing it gently with his teeth, worrying it softly and with exquisite care.

"Sean," she shrieked, clamping her legs against his invading hand.

He felt her vagina expand as though she was trying to thrust his fingers from inside her then the walls quivered in a succession of tightening and release that almost felt as though she was attempting to swallow his hand, to snatch it up inside her cunt.

He pushed his fingers deeper, striving to touch her very womb, and the intensity of her orgasm brought a scream from her throat. Knowing he had not hurt her but given her a climax to equal—or exceed—any she had ever experienced, he smiled, keeping his fingers deep inside her.

She shuddered one last time then fell limp, her head lolling to one side, her chest heaving as she struggled to draw the air into lungs she had been denied for the duration of her orgasm. Her legs relaxed then splayed open, leaving her helpless and exposed.

"Mine," he said, easing his fingers from inside her.

"Yours," she whispered in reply.

He gathered her into his arms, stretched his long body out beside hers and placed a chaste kiss on her forehead.

"Sleep, my lady," he said.

As soul-numbing peace settled over Kiley Trevor, she could hear his strong, steady heartbeat. She could feel his warm flesh molded to hers. She could smell the spent juices of their bodies mixed with the heady cologne he wore. She could sense the pleasure he felt because she knew her own had given her a glimpse into heaven.

Long into the night as the woman in his arms slept soundly, contentedly, Julian St. John stared up into the flickering lights of the tree headboard. Gone was the peace of the moment that had given him more pleasure than he had ever thought possible. In its place were plans on how he would keep this woman safe and with him forever.

Chapter Ten

Celeste Dubois threw the porcelain vase against the wall as hard as she could. Her black eyes were flashing with fury, her scarlet lips skinned back over pearly white teeth that were clenched tightly together. Digging half-moon wounds into her palms, her manicured nails drew blood.

"I'll be damned if I'll let that bitch reveal his true identity. That bastard in England will find out where he is. I won't allow that to happen," she swore.

"What would you like me to do?" Pierce Umsted, her personal assistant, inquired.

"Get my jet ready and let Julian know I will be waiting for his yacht to pick me up in Kingston," Celeste grated.

"Yes, ma'am," Pierce agreed and picked up the phone to call his employer's pilot. He spoke quietly into the phone, giving instructions to the Learjet pilot. When he was finished, he hung up and turned around to face his employer. "Anything else, ma'am?"

"Julian forgets himself sometimes," Celeste stated. "He doesn't take his personal safety all that seriously. He thinks he's safe on the Cay but they can get to him."

Pierce nodded in agreement.

Stamping her foot, Celeste jerked her head, flinging her long hair over her shoulder. "I get so frustrated with that boy."

"I know you do," Pierce soothed, going to his employer and taking her into his arms.

She knew in her heart that the woman Julian chose was the one he wanted and needed. As long as she was good to him, she'd let Kiley Trevor keep breathing. The moment she hurt Julian, she would be gone.

Celeste knew this day would come and a part of her had wanted it to. Julian deserved to be happy. His life had been a true horror before she came along. She wanted the best for him, and if the Trevor woman was who he wanted, Celeste would make sure Julian got his love. As long as the bitch didn't give away his identity or hurt him Celeste would stay out of his affairs.

But that did not stop her from loving Julian St. John with all her heart.

She settled into her assistant's arms, nestling her cheek against his broad chest. She sighed. "Next to Julian, you are the next best thing, do you know that, Pierce?"

Pierce stroked Celeste's long hair. "I try, ma'am," he said, his eyes hard as blue flint.

"Fuck me," Celeste commanded, digging her nails into Pierce's chest. "And make it good."

He swung her into his arms and took her to her bed, dropping her upon the mattress as though she was a sack of salt. Though she tried to turn to her side, he jerked her to her back and grabbed the front of her expensive Parisian gown. With a grunt, he ripped the bodice open—mindless of her nails streaking down his forearms.

She fought him like a banshee—cursing, spitting, kicking. His superior strength did not allow her to wiggle from the bed and his rock-hard body straddled hers, ripping away her undergarments, cruelly kneading the bare breasts that thrust from the torn fabric of her chemise. His rough hands batted hers away.

"Whore," he recited from between clenched teeth. "Don't you dare fight me, you slut."

It was a game they played, both reveling in their positions. When he used a scrap of her once beautiful gown to tie her wrists to the headboard, he pulled the material tight enough to bruise her flesh.

"Please," she begged, tears gathering in her eyes. "Don't do this."

"Shut up," he growled and lifted her legs so her knees pressed firmly to her chest. He anchored them there with his shoulders as he fumbled with the zipper of his slacks.

Thrusting into her with a brutal force that pushed her higher in the bed, he slammed into her viciously.

"You are hurting me," she cried out, pulling against her bonds.

"You haven't seen hurt yet, bitch," he warned.

He splayed her legs apart and grabbed her breasts, savagely squeezing them. His fingernails plucked at her nipples, gouging into them, twisting the tender flesh until she screamed with the pain.

"That's it," he crooned in an evil voice. "Let me hear you scream again."

He bent forward and took one engorged nipple between his teeth, biting hard enough to draw blood. The sound that came from

Celeste's throat made him laugh as he sucked hard on the wounded protrusion.

"Julian, please," Celeste whimpered. "Be gentle with me."

* * * * *

Sheer fury filled Pierce's soul at the mention of his hated enemy. He slid his mouth farther up her breast and bit into the quivering flesh, leaving deep teeth prints in the full globe. Celeste's shriek of agony was like music to his ears and he slammed into her with renewed force.

"Pierce," he snarled. "My name is Pierce."

Celeste wobbled her head back and forth on the rumpled coverlet. Her fantasy lover was not the former college football player who arched over her. The lover of her dreams, the man of her heart, was a thousand miles away, lying in the arms of another woman.

"Julian," she cried, tears falling down her cheeks, ruining her expertly applied makeup.

"Pierce," her tormentor spat. He dragged his nails down the tender insides of her thighs, pushing them so far apart he knew he was close to breaking her pelvis.

As he rode her, plowing into her channel as though he was trying to thrust his cock into her throat, he sunk his teeth into the already scarred flesh of her shoulder until he tasted the sweet saltiness of her blood.

"Julian," Celeste whispered as he felt her climax at the inner lining of her cunt.

They came together—he, jamming his hard cock as brutally as he could, she, straining upward to catch every last spurt of his essence and the last cruel thrust of pain. As her satiation culminated, she shouted Julian's name.

"You bitch," he swore, hating her at the same time he gently untied her hands from the headboard. "My name is Pierce."

Celeste gathered him to her, cradling his sweaty body to hers. She smoothed her palms over the muscles of his back.

"I know who you are," she said softly.

"I love you," he told her.

"Yes, I know," she crooned, rocking him in her arms.

"More than he ever will."

Celeste shrugged. "I fear that is true."

Pierce craned his neck to look up into her beautiful face. "Then why do you deny me?"

"Because," she said, lowering her head to plant a gentle kiss on his damp brow, "you aren't Julian and it is Julian I want."

Hurt drove deep in Pierce's heart and he slumped against her, burying his face in her shoulder. No matter what he did, it was never enough. No matter how much he hurt her, shamed her, did her bidding, he always came up short in her eyes.

Long after Celeste was asleep, Pierce lay awake plotting vicious brutalities, creating savage fantasies of his own.

And none of them involved the luscious woman lying beside him.

Chapter Eleven

Clive Bellington shot the cuffs of his expensive suit then adjusted his cravat. He turned sideways to admire himself in the full-length mirror and, apparently satisfied with his appearance, he turned away.

"But how long will you be gone, dear?" Edwina Bellington stood just inside her lover's bedroom door, twisting a handkerchief between her arthritic fingers.

"I have no idea," Clive replied, allowing his manservant to assist him with putting on a cashmere overcoat. "You know how those Americans can be."

Edwina lifted the handkerchief to dab at her eyes. "I will miss you." She smiled hesitantly. "It wouldn't take me long to throw a bag together."

Clive rolled his eyes. "We've been over this ad nauseum, Winnie. You would only be bored. When I return, we'll have a holiday in Capri. How does that sound?"

Sighing, Edwina tucked the handkerchief into the pocket of her silk dressing gown. It was obvious to her Clive did not want her along on this trip.

Not that he ever took her on his trips to America.

"It's been so long since I was in the Colonies," she said in a wistful tone. "I rather liked Chicago."

"Well, it isn't like it was thirty-odd years ago," Clive replied. "Not like it was when you and Albert were there."

At the mention of her late husband—Clive's older brother— Edwina hung her head. Her one short year in Chicago with the man she had been forced to marry had not been as pleasant as she had led everyone to believe. Had she been with Clive, the man she had wanted and still loved more than anything else in her life, her stay in America would have been sheer bliss. She would not have wanted to return to England though she knew Clive's heart was rooted firmly in the foggy country.

"Perhaps you will take me with you when you go next time?" she asked hopefully.

"Perhaps," Clive mumbled, eying his manservant who would be accompanying him on the trip. He walked to her and graced her with a quick peck of a kiss. "Be good now," he ordered.

From his bedroom window, three stories up from the sweeping turnaround in front of the Bellington mansion, Edwina watched Clive being ushered into the town car that would take him to a private airport outside London. She traced a random pattern on the window glass as she leaned her head against the pane. Her heart lurched as the town car pulled away.

When Albert had been found slumped over his desk that cold February morning twenty-five years earlier, Edwina had expected Clive to ask her to marry him after a decent interval of mourning Albert's loss had passed. But no matter how she hinted that such a thing was her fondest wish, Clive seemed not to notice. He was content to live with her in his own set of elegant apartments in the mansion and come to her bed in the dark of night, never showing his affection in public. Only their servants—as discreet as any Englishman or woman had ever been—knew the true nature of their relationship.

The town car disappeared beyond the tall yews at the end of the estate's serpentine driveway and Edwina walked to Clive's bed. She pulled the silk coverlet aside and stretched out upon the crisp linen sheets. She stroked Clive's pillow, pressing her cheek into the smell of him, inhaling his essence.

* * * * *

"Did you let Morris know I would like the prime rib for dinner tomorrow evening?" Clive asked Hansen, his manservant.

"Yes, milord," Hansen replied. "And he has laid in a stock of your favorite ale."

"Excellent," Clive said. "It will be nice to be away from the estate for a few days."

Hansen smiled.

"I detest having to meet with that Umsted chap," Clive complained. "He is such a boor."

Hansen nodded. No reply was expected of him.

"He did say he would take me to Julian this time," Clive commented. "That will make this trip less taxing."

"Indeed, milord," Hansen agreed.

"We will find a way to bring Julian to justice," Clive said. "All we need do is get him off that despicable island of his." He turned to look out his window. "Once he is behind bars and sitting on death row, I can breathe easier."

Hansen shifted uncomfortably on the seat, bringing Clive's attention to him.

"The piles bothering you again, old man?" Clive asked with a smirk.

Hansen ducked his head. "I am afraid so, milord."

Clive picked up his umbrella and poked the driver in the back. "Find a loo for us, Richards."

Hansen shifted again, pulling a face that suggested he was in major discomfort.

A few meters down the road, Richards turned into a petrol station and parked. He got out to open the door for Hansen, a servant higher up the ranks than himself.

Hansen smiled apologetically, thanked his employer and exited the car, walking as stiff-cheeked as he could into the station.

The attendant glanced up then went back to reading the *London Times* as Hansen headed for the telephone kiosk.

A call was placed to a number in Birmingham. A single word was spoken to the woman who answered at the other end. Before the town car wound its way to the private airport from which Clive and Hansen would be winging to America, word had been passed onto a number on Mistral Cay.

*****

"Boogeyman," Henri wrote in his ever-present notebook.

Chapter Twelve

"Tell me what happened," Kiley asked.

Julian sighed heavily. "Why do you want to know?"

"I want to know everything about you," she said.

He shifted so they were lying with her in his arms, his front to her backside, snug as spoons in a kitchen drawer.

"It's not something I talk about," he told her.

"Why did that man try to kill you?" she asked to encourage him.

Julian was silent for a long time, his breathing audible in her ear. She knew he was awake, forming the words in his mind before he shared them with her. She waited, not pressing, her hands lightly clutching his arms, one thumb rubbing the wiry hair on his wrist.

"I left home when I was twelve," he said. "It was after the Christmas holiday and I was on my way back to the boarding school where my father had gone when he was a boy. I had tampered with the stem on the tire, figuring about how long it would take the sedan to get to a stretch of road far enough away from any nearby houses." He chuckled. "I've always been good at math."

"I haven't," Kiley laughed in reply.

"While the chauffer was changing the tire, I got out and told him I had to take a leak."

"And never came back."

"And never came back," Julian echoed.

"Where on earth does a twelve-year-old boy go when he's running away?"

"To the docks," Julian answered. "And a ship onto which I could stow away."

"That was a dangerous thing to do."

"More dangerous than I realized," Julian agreed. "I hid inside a crate, thinking I would be able to sneak out at night and find something to eat." He snorted. "I wasn't counting on that crate being shoved up against several others with no way for me to get out."

She gasped. "Oh, my God. You could have starved to death." Her eyes widened. "Or suffocated."

"I realized that a bit too late," he said.

"Just thinking about it scares me," she said, tears gathering.

"I have nightmares about it," he told her. "Henri has told me I wake up clawing at the air." He shrugged. "I guess I'm trying to claw my way out of the crate. I don't know."

"You traveled all the way to America like that?" she asked.

"Yes," he answered. "If it hadn't have been for Henri, I probably wouldn't be here today."

"He found you," she stated.

"He smelled me," Julian corrected.

He went on to tell her how Henri had been snooping around the docks, looking for something to steal, and had caught a whiff of the smell of excrement coming from a crate containing boxes of prams—English baby carriages. Of how Henri had used a forklift to move aside the crate jammed in front of the one in which Julian hid and how he had pried open the crate only to catch an unconscious, starving boy in his arms.

"He thought an animal had somehow gotten into the crate. Henri is a staunch animal activist and he didn't stop to think what he was doing when he illegally opened that crate. It never occurred to him he'd find a human in there," Julian said. He sighed. "A half-starved boy at that."

"What did he do?" she asked. "Did he turn you in?"

"No, that wouldn't have occurred to Henri, either," Julian replied.

"He took you in," she said.

"He took me to Celeste. He was working for her at the time."

Kiley bristled at the name. "Did she pay him to provide boys for her brothel?" she grumbled.

"Henri had numerous ways of making money back then, sweetness. He is a pickpocket of the first order as well as one hell of a cat burglar, a master forger and the best card shark I've ever seen. He is also quite the enforcer when he needs to be."

"Did Celeste Dubois pay him to provide males for her brothels?" Kiley repeated.

Julian tightened his hold around her. "As a matter of fact, yes."

"Son of a bitch," she fumed. "I knew there was a reason I didn't like that man."

"He didn't procure them for her, sweetness," Julian said. "He introduced them to her. What they did after that was their affair."

"Yeah, well, did she pay him for those introductions?"

When Julian didn't answer right away, she craned her neck and looked up at him. The glow of the tinkling lights in the branches overhead shone in his eyes.

"Well? Did she?"

Julian let out a long breath. "Yes, she did."

"Then he procured for her," she said.

Not wanting to argue with her, he nuzzled her neck. "She's not as bad as you think she is, Kiley."

"So he took you to her," she said, ignoring his assessment of the woman. "And she nursed you back to health." Her words were said in a mocking tone.

"You were asking about the man I killed," he reminded her. "Not my introduction to Celeste."

"And in gratitude, you became one of her male escorts," she said, pretending not to take the hint.

"You want to know about that?" he asked, his tone as sharp as hers had been mocking.

"How much did she charge for you at that age?"

Julian squeezed his eyes shut. "Kiley, she never sold me to other women. She didn't even touch me until she considered me old enough. By then, I'd gotten over the reason I'd run away in the first place."

"Which was what, exactly?"

"My uncle and adoptive father molesting me," he replied.

She tried to turn over in his arms, wanting to face him but he wouldn't allow it. He kept her back to him.

"D-did your mother know?" she asked.

"No, I don't think she ever did. They were careful to hide it from her. I don't even think she suspected they were abusing me."

He told her of his childhood. Of how his father and uncle had hurt him, degraded him, abused him in ways he could not discuss. Of how he had tried twice before to run away only to be caught and punished in such a brutal manner he had spent several days in bed. Of how his mother had stood by witnessing his chastisement that day, unaware of the real reason he was being punished. He told her of his misery and his self-loathing and how he felt unloved and unwanted. Of how his mother often ignored him most of the time, foisting him off on the servants to be cared for.

"I spent a lot of time by myself when my father and uncle were in London on business. I would go out to the woods and lay under this old tree, staring up through the branches, watching the fireflies."

"That's why you had this bed built?"

"It was the one place I felt safe," he replied.

She clutched his arms, trying to pass her sympathy onto him in touch.

"Celeste took care of me," he explained. "She showed me the love I had not known since I was a small boy."

"I'm sure your mother loved you in her way," she said.

"My real mother, yes," he said quietly. "Not the one who adopted me."

The knowledge of who was lying beside her surged through Kiley's mind like a freight train speeding through the night. She jerked around, pulling out of his arms, sitting up to stare down at him. "You're...you're..."

"Patrick Sean O'Reilly," he said in way of an acknowledgment. "If you really want to see the birthmark, I'll be happy to show it to you."

"You knew all along why I was here," she accused. "You knew your mother was looking for you."

"Not exactly," he defended. "I knew I was adopted but never knew who my birth parents were. I certainly didn't know she was looking for me. If I had, I would have contacted her long before now."

"But you knew why I was here," she said.

"Something didn't sound right with the background information Dr. Carstairs provided us. I had Henri check you out. That's when he found out who you worked for, why you were at the Cay and who had hired you."

"How did you learn all that?" she said, her brows slanted.

"Ross Bennis really likes his bourbon, doesn't he? Buy him enough shots and he'll tell you who shot Kennedy, I imagine."

"Son of a bitch," Kiley mumbled. "Greg needs to find a new partner."

"Greg needs his ass kicked," Julian growled.

"Well at least it didn't come as too much of a shock for you," she said, ignoring his remark. "I guess your adoptive parents had told you already that you were adopted."

He shook his head. "Oh, no. They would never have admitted something like that. It wasn't in their best interests for anyone— especially me—to know I wasn't their real son."

"How did you find out then?"

"By eavesdropping," he admitted. "And it's true what they say—an eavesdropper never hears anything good about themselves when they sneak around and listen in where they shouldn't."

She touched his face. "What did they say?"

"I believe my father's exact words were, 'I didn't want the brat to begin with. I despise the little bastard. I can't wait to get him out of our lives.'"

"Oh, baby," Kiley said, her throat clogging with tears. "How old were you?"

"Eight, nine," he answered. "Old enough to understand what it meant when my mother said they should have gone to an English orphanage instead of an American one because an English boy would have suited them better."

"How awful that must have been for you," Kiley whispered.

"I don't know if I was more upset at learning I was adopted or that I was a Yank," he said with a snort.

"Why did they come to America?" she queried. "How could an English couple—?"

"I didn't learn the particulars of my adoption until I met Celeste. She hired a private investigator to look into it. He couldn't find out who my real parents were because he never found any records of my birth. I suspect Albert paid enough money under the table for those records to disappear. I don't know where I was born—"

"Iowa," Kiley supplied. "Riverside, to be precise. Future birthplace of Captain James T. Kirk."

Julian groaned. "A Midwesterner. How unsophisticated can one get?"

Kiley punched him lightly. "Hey, I was born in Council Bluffs, Iowa."

"The detective Celeste hired went to England and, after spreading around a rather large sum of money, gathered quite a bit of information from Bellington servants." He chuckled nastily. "Albert must have been rolling in his grave when those servants gave out information I'm sure neither he nor his brother knew they were privy to. I wasn't the only one listening at keyholes."

They were silent for a moment then she asked how he came to be adopted.

"Albert Bellington's family knew what he was. He was head over heels in debt, very close to being sent to jail for buggering little boys. His grandfather found him a bride, Edwina Cullford Simpson, and forced him to marry her. Edwina was in love with Albert's brother Clive but Clive was no different than his older brother—a sodomite of the highest order. Edwina was the heir to a vast fortune and both brothers needed that money. They wanted a baronial estate, money to spend lavishly on their male lovers and the respect being allied to the Simpson name could give them. As a wedding present Edwina's parents gave her a mansion Albert promptly named Bellington Hall and Clive moved in with them."

"Were they…. Did they…?" Kiley bit her lip, unsure of how to ask the question that nauseated her.

"I always thought so but I don't know for sure," Julian replied.

"Albert didn't love his wife, I take it," she said.

"He despised her."

"And she loved Clive."

"To this day I doubt she knows he prefers males."

"Then why did they want children?"

"Edwina was an only child. At her father's death, she inherited a vast amount of money. There was money in the Bellington family as well. More than in the Simpson's but Albert's grandfather refused to give either of his sons the inheritance because he knew they would go through it like a hot knife through butter. The only way Albert would ever see the Simpson money was to produce a male heir for his grandfather."

"Edwina couldn't have children?"

"Didn't want to," Julian told her. "So they took an extended holiday in America, privately looking for a child to adopt." He clenched his teeth. "Lucky me that they found me, huh?"

"I'm surprised Albert's grandfather didn't object."

Julian laughed mirthlessly. "He never knew," he said. "The Bellington family was told Edwina was expecting and the physician warned travel was not recommended. That is why she supposedly gave birth in the States rather than in England." He plowed a hand through his thick black hair. "She and Albert took pictures of her with a pillow under maternity dresses so the old man could see her in the family way. Albert's grandfather passed away before the happy event took place."

"That is awful," Kiley proclaimed.

"It was in the will that the heir to the Bellington estate was to inherit on his twenty-first birthday. If that heir died before inheriting, the money would go to numerous charities. If he died after inheriting the estate, his next of kin—meaning my father—would get eighty percent of the money." He sighed deeply. "I doubt I would have survived all that long after I inherited."

Kiley's eyes widened. "You think they would have had you murdered?"

"That's exactly what they tried when they sent that man after me in New Orleans."

He told of opening his door one evening to find Clive standing there with another man. The shock of seeing his "uncle" was surpassed only by the attempt on his life.

"I had turned twenty-one a few months earlier. How they found me, I have no idea. Apparently Clive wanted to make sure I never saw a penny of the money I was entitled to. His hired killer came after me with a knife as good old Clive stood there watching, smiling like a jackal." Julian scooted up in the bed, leaning back against the wide headboard that resembled a thick tree trunk. "They didn't count on me knowing how to use a knife, too."

It had been Celeste who had taught him many things as he grew up—how to make love to a woman, how to run a brothel, how to protect himself. Henri had helped him to hone his skills, teaching him dirty tricks even Celeste didn't know.

"I never went anywhere without a switchblade. New Orleans's red-light district isn't a particularly safe place. Clive's killer and I fought; I wound up gutting him and would have gone after Clive, too, but the son of a bitch stabbed me in the back with his knife he took out of my kitchen while I was fighting with the man."

"You lost a kidney," she said softly.

"I almost lost my life," he countered. "I think he thought he'd killed me." He narrowed his eyes. "He should have stayed around long enough to make sure."

"Lucky for you he didn't," she reminded him.

"Henri found me and took me to the doctor Celeste used to take care of her employees. Within an hour, I was on her jet and on the way to Jamaica where I had the surgery."

"She covered up your murder of the—"

"No, she never had a chance to. She would have if she could have but Clive called the cops and they were all over my apartment before Celeste's plane ever left the runway. A warrant was issued for my arrest and he told them he would testify I attacked the man without provocation. That's why I can't ever go back to the States."

"She brought you here."

He nodded. "She owned the island back then. We've since worked out a deal whereby I purchased the Cay from her. I've owned it for the last fifteen years."

"I can only imagine the price you paid for it," she muttered.

Julian grinned. "I suppose you can but you'd most likely be wrong."

"You aren't lovers?" she demanded.

"We have been. I won't lie to you about that, but I haven't lain with her in over six months. I had decided to end it a year before that." He shrugged. "But she can be a very persuasive woman."

"I'll just bet she can," Kiley said, her mouth twisted.

"I was waiting for you," he told her.

"You didn't even know me," she countered.

"No, but I knew I'd recognize you when we met."

"You—"

"Shush," he said, reaching out to cup her cheek "The past—yours and mine—is in the past. From this day forward, it will be just the two of us."

"You don't think she'll try to keep you?" she asked. "I know I would if I was her."

"She'll be happy for me," he said, pulling Kiley toward him. His lips closed over hers, drowning out any further words she would have spoken.

As his body slid over hers, his hands molding her body to his, the phone on the bedside table chimed softly.

They ignored it.

Chapter Thirteen

Henri put the receiver down and stood tapping his pen against his lips. Julian needed to know his uncle was on his way to meet with Celeste, but he would also need to be told they had an informer in the Bellington household. Until now, Henri had seen no reason to tell Julian that tabs were being kept on the family. For Julian's safety, that had been a decision Henri had made himself several years earlier.

"You've learned about Miss Trevor and you don't like it, eh, Celeste?" Henri said aloud.

"Why do you suppose she contacted his uncle?" Christian, Julian's housekeeper inquired. He was sitting with his feet propped up on the corner of Henri's desk, sipping a Manhattan.

Henri frowned. Sometimes he forgot Christian was about. He looked thoughtfully at the man who had been his lover for the last twelve years. "I don't remember telling you that she had."

Christian's eyes shifted away from Henri's. "You must have," he said, flicking lint from his white linen britches. "How else would I have known?"

"How else, indeed?" Henri replied. He sat down at his desk and uncapped his Mont Blanc to write something in his notebook. He looked at the word and smiled slowly.

"Henri?" Christian inquired. "You didn't answer me."

Recapping his pen, Henri leaned back in the chair, rolling the gold cylinder between his index fingers and thumbs. "Why do I think she contacted Clive Bellington?"

Christian nodded as he took another sip of his drink.

Henri latched his eyes on Christian and began to fashion a tale he thought would sound plausible.

"Well, I imagine she thinks she will be able to find a way to get Julian onboard his yacht and off the island. If she can get him to Kingston, she can have good old Clive threaten him into being a good little boy. Perhaps Clive will make threats against Miss Trevor. Since Julian has become enthralled with the lady, I'm sure he'd do most anything to keep her safe, don't you?" He cocked his head to one side. "How do you suppose Celeste found out about Miss Trevor, Christy?"

Christian tipped his head back and drained his drink. He put his feet down on the floor and shook his head. "I can't begin to guess," he said, getting up. He walked to the bar to fix another Manhattan.

"It seems our mole has been at work again, doesn't it?" Henri asked, watching as Christian's hands shook as he poured liquor into his glass.

"Yes, it would seem so."

Henri looked out the window. "Well, I guess I'll have to step up my efforts at finding out who that rat is." He glanced down at his notebook. The word "mole" stared back at him.

"If I can be of any help, just ask," Christian told him, taking his seat once again.

Taking up his notebook, Henri pushed back from desk. He slid his pen into his pocket. "I believe I left that new Arkenstone CD down at our little hideaway. Would you be a dear and get it for me?"

"Now?" Christian asked. He glanced at the window. "It's pitch dark out there."

Henri smiled. "I really want to play it when we retire tonight. It really sets the mood for great lovemaking, don't you think?"

Christian sighed. "All right," he agreed. Once more he drained his glass and got to his feet. "But you'll have to make it up to me for that long trek down the bloody beach, Henri."

"I'll pay you back for everything you've done, my dear. Have no fear of that," Henri said. "Now, I really need to talk to Julian. Since he isn't answering his phone, I'll have to interrupt his little tête-à-tête."

"He won't like it," Christian warned as Henri opened the door.

"No," Henri agreed. "He isn't going to like what I have to tell him at all."

Walking down the corridor, Henri's face was hard, his eyes steely as he stopped before Julian's office and punched in the security key code. Once inside, he picked up the house phone.

"There is a matter I need you to take care of for me," he told the man who answered. "Be careful you aren't seen and I don't want any evidence of tonight's work to come bobbing up at the beach."

"Who am I to cancel?" the man inquired.

"He's on his way to my cottage down the beach. Take care of the matter as he's returning to the resort."

"Any other instructions, sir?"

"Yes. Make sure the CD he will be carrying isn't damaged and bring it to me."

* * * * *

The light knocks on the door to the Forest Room suite were repeated three times, a signal to Julian who it was that was intruding on his private time. They were also an indication to the resort's owner that it was a matter of some importance.

Padding softly to the door so as not to awaken Kiley, Julian opened the portal quietly, standing aside so Henri could slip inside.

"What's wrong?" Julian asked quietly.

"Our mole," Henri whispered, "was Christian."

Julian lowered his head and stood there arms akimbo. "You're sure?"

"Without a single doubt," Henri answered.

Lifting his head, Julian stared at his old friend. "I'm sorry, Henri. I know you two are—"

"Were," Henri interrupted. He shrugged. "Perhaps I meant something to him, perhaps not. It might all have simply been a guise to learn all he could from someone close to you." He squeezed his eyes closed. "Forgive me, Julian."

"For what?" Julian asked. Before Henri could protest, he reached out to grip the man's shoulders. "You saved my life not once but twice, old friend. You helped Celeste get documents for me with the name Julian St. John on them. As far as the American government believed, that was who I was."

"They know your real name now, Julian," Henri reminded him. He ground his teeth. "Thanks to Clive Bellington."

"That doesn't matter. I won't ever leave Mistral Cay."

"Celeste had that pretty boy of hers call us this evening. She is on her way down to Kingston and wants you to send the yacht for her." He held up his hand before Julian could ask why. "And Bellington is on his way here as well."

"Pierce told you that?" Julian asked, his face tight with alarm.

"I have a man at Bellington Hall," Henri admitted. "He phoned to tell me Clive is on the way here."

Julian removed his hands from Henri's shoulders. "Do you think Celeste was responsible for Clive finding me the first time?" he asked.

Henri cocked one shoulder. "I don't think so, but who knows?" He thought about it for a moment. "No, I'm fairly sure she didn't because she didn't want to lose you. She doesn't want to lose you now and I think that's why Bellington was told where you are."

"But why?" Julian asked, raising his voice. Remembering Kiley was in the next room, he lowered his next words to a near whisper. "She knows Clive wants me dead. She knows he'd like nothing better than to see me in prison, awaiting my execution. Why would she tell him?"

"She didn't," Henri said. "But I believe I know who did."

"Pierce."

"Yeah. That little bugger hates you as much as he loves Celeste."

"He doesn't love her as much as he wants her business," Julian replied.

"That's probably true," Henri agreed. "But he poses a danger to her as much as the danger he poses for you."

"I can handle Pierce."

"I know you can and we need to nip what the little bastard has started in the bud."

"Which is what?"

"Keeping Miss Trevor safe?" Henri suggested.

Julian stared at him.

"If Pierce told Clive where you are, chances are good he would have told him about Miss Trevor as well. Clive could hire a woman professional to take Miss Trevor out. She'd be just one more client suggested and vouched for by one of our clients Clive can find a way to get to," Henri explained. "It wouldn't be hard to do, Julian, and he knows how much that would hurt you."

Julian's gaze shifted slowly to the bedroom door. His heart was lying in that room.

"I warned you long ago we should cancel Clive Bellington. Now is as good a time as any," Henri said. When Julian looked at him, Henri lifted a brow. "Do you want to keep looking over your shoulder, wondering if that next client is the one who'll harm your lady?"

"I don't want Celeste here," Julian said. "Phone Umsted. Tell him now isn't a good time for her to come calling. Make sure our yacht doesn't leave the harbor and have the chopper out patrolling. If Bellington tries to barge his way in here, tell Jonesy to blow the damned boat out of the water."

"He'd have to be inside the three-mile limit first," Henri warned.

"Fine," Julian snapped.

"I'll tell Umsted what will happen if he should try to sail here. My guess is he'll get word to Bellington."

"Just keep him from the Cay." Julian ordered.

Chapter Fourteen

Julian slipped back into the bed, his mind roiling with turmoil. He was cold, his heart pounding and his hands clammy as he lay down, trying not to awaken Kiley who lay with her back to him.

"Who was at the door?" she asked sleepily. She turned over and nestled against him, lifting her head so he could slide his arm beneath her neck.

"Just Henri," he answered. He wanted no secrets or lies between them as they began their journey through life together but neither did he want to alarm her. There were things she did not need to know. "It was Cay business."

"Um," Kiley mumbled as she slid her hand down his chest to pluck at the thick, wiry curls on his abdomen. "You tired?"

Julian smiled. "Not anymore," he replied, putting his hand over hers and lowering her fingers to his cock. "You have a knack for taking my mind off my troubles."

"Is something bothering you?"

"We'll talk about it later," he responded, easing his arm out from beneath her. He turned over and slid down the mattress, shoving the coverlet aside as he moved.

His hands were on her hips, his face pressing against her belly as he placed light kisses around her navel. She sucked in her breath as his tongue delved into the concavity. She wiggled against the invasion and buried her fingers in his dark curls. Her breathing increased as he circled her navel with the tip of his tongue then began a downward trail of wet heat onto her pubic mound.

Julian slid his hand between her legs then upward as he cupped her buttocks, bringing her hips up as he lifted. She brought her feet to his shoulders, bracing her instep on his collarbones to give him access to that part of her he sought.

He was burning for her as he placed a gentle kiss along the entrance to her core. His breath moved over the sensitive pubic hair and he felt her shiver. She clutched his hair, pressing him closer to her, and when his lips touched her most responsive place, she moaned with pleasure, closing her eyes against the flick of his tongue against her.

He circled the straining little nub, lashed it lovingly from side to side then licked at it with short, upward strokes that made her pant. His fingers dug gently into her rump, anchoring her as he nipped at that receptive piece of flesh.

"Oh, God," she cried and he could feel her legs trembling.

His short upward stroke lengthened until he was lapping her from the base of her lips to the top. A trickle of her essence oozed onto his chin as he lapped at the musky taste. The smell of her was invading his senses, stiffening an erection already as hard as he could ever remember it being. His tumescence was almost painful—certainly insistent—but her pleasure meant more to him at that moment and he eased one hand out from under her so he could peel back the hood that covered her clitoris. When his tongue touched the ultra-aware protrusion, she arched her hips upward.

He knew what she needed and slid his fingers into her moist opening. She was hot, oozing with need and as he moved his fingers inside her, the middle finger stroking her G-spot, he heard her moaning, felt the movement as she tossed her head from side to side.

"Come, sweetness," he whispered. "Give me your juice. Let me taste you."

His words were like a prod, spurring her closer to fulfillment. She strained against him as his fingers pressed deeply within her. But it was not until he turned his palm downward, rotating his fingers inside her and slipped his thumb into her anus that waves of pure ecstasy broke over her and she screamed with the intensity of her climax.

She came with quick little waves of tightening that captured his fingers. Three rapid constrictions then two slower ones then finally one less strong convulsion that left her limp upon the bed, her hands fallen away from his hair where only a moment before she had nearly pulled those strands from their roots with the power of her release. Her legs quivered as he gently lowered them from his shoulders.

"Take me," she pleaded, her breaths no less slow than they had been before she climaxed.

He slid into her, going in to the very root of him, and held his hard erection against her. As he slowly began to move inside her, she lifted her hands and clutched at his shoulders.

Once more he put his hands beneath her hips and lifted her to him, going as deep inside her as he could. With slow, sure strokes he pressed into her then sped up his invasion as his blood began to boil with the urgent need to spill his seed.

After years of learning to control his body for pleasure, this woman undid him and he lost it, plunging into her with everything he had. Finally he pushed all the way into her and held his cock there as he spurted, the jerking movement of his shaft accompanying his roar of release.

Her legs wrapped around his waist, imprisoning him to her as he collapsed upon her, his sweaty chest slick against her breasts. Her arms were around his shoulders. He had been seeking this completion all his life.

"Never leave me," Julian whispered. His cheek was pressed to her chest.

"Never," she vowed as she raised her head and kissed his hair. She lay down then pulled him against her, her breathing slowing to normal.

They fell asleep in that position—his head on her breast, her arms holding him to her, the fingers of her hand threaded through his dark hair.

* * * * *

When they woke, the sun was streaming through the window and the smell of coffee wafted to them from the living area of the suite.

Julian rolled over to his back, and flung arm over his eyes. Kiley left the comfort of the bed and padded to the bathroom. When she had relieved herself and washed her face, she fetched the coffee that had been left on a silver tray along with a bud vase that held a single crimson rose.

"Tell me he left croissants, too," Julian mumbled.

"He left croissants, but let's have a cup of coffee first," she replied as she placed the tray on a nearby table.

Pushing himself up in the bed, Julian took the steaming cup of coffee she held out to him, inhaling its rich aroma before cautiously taking a sip. He liked his brew dark, without sugar or cream, but he could smell the rich scent of vanilla and knew Henri had provided Kiley with what she liked.

She climbed onto the bed with her cup and sat cross-legged, totally at ease with his and her nudity. She closed her eyes to the heady taste of the strong coffee. "French vanilla," she sighed. "I love it."

"He knew."

"There are huge strawberries, melon slices, too. Enough to feed five people."

Julian laughed. "Henri believes you should be nourished after a long night of love."

"He's right," Kiley said. "I'm famished."

He took a long sip of his coffee, burning his mouth a bit in the process, but held her gaze. There were things that had to be said.

"Can I see it?" she asked.

He blinked. "See what?"

Kiley giggled like a teenage girl. "The birthmark, silly."

Julian rolled his eyes kicked aside the sheet covering his lower legs then spread them. "Be my guest."

She set her cup on the bedside table and came to kneel between his legs. Like a shy, virginal wife, she bent forward, lifted his penis and found what she had been sent to the Cay to find. She looked up at him. "It more resembles a crossbow than an anchor," she told him.

He hooted with laughter. "A crossbow?"

"Well, both are attached to a long shaft," she laughed.

"Brazen hussy," he pronounced. "Come here."

She retrieved her cup and settled against him, his strong arm loosely draped over her shoulder. "She really wants to hear from you."

He knew whom she meant. "I spoke to her yesterday but I'm not so sure that was a wise thing to have done."

"Why not?"

"She has blood pressure problems and I think I scared her."

"Well, we'll call back today and you two can set up a place to meet and—"

"I can't leave here," he reminded her.

"No, but she could come to the Cay."

"Hell, no," he snapped, one leg jerking with annoyance. "Would you invite *your* mother here?"

Kiley made a rude sound. "Might be just what she needs," she responded.

"It isn't what my mother needs," he told her, relaxing a bit.

"Then where?" she asked and then turned to him. "How 'bout aboard your yacht?"

He thought about it for a moment. It wasn't such a bad idea. He could send a jet for his mother, bring her to Kingston where she could board the yacht that brought clients to the Cay. He could then rendezvous with her on his own yacht.

"As long as we stay inside the three-mile limit," he said slowly, remembering his last conversation with Henri.

"Then call her," Kiley insisted. "Don't waste any time."

For a moment he considered doing as she suggested but the matter of Celeste and her machinations needed to be dealt with first. He did not need to have his mother meet the infamous madam in Kingston.

"I'd like to talk with her a few times before we actually meet," he said.

She could sense his nervousness, could feel his embarrassment. "She killed a man, too," she said and watched as he turned to stare at her, his lips open. She nodded. "Your father."

The tale took nearly an hour to tell. Kiley wanted to make sure she related all the details she had read from Fay O'Reilly's file. From the day the high school freshman had met Jason Faulkner to the day she found out she was carrying his child—a child Jason did not want.

"She was fifteen years old when he seduced her," Kiley explained. "She was camping at the Iowa State Fair with her brothers and father while they were showing their sheep for judging. Faulkner was a carnie worker, hawking tickets for one of the rides. He was eighteen and according to what she told Bennis, he was as handsome as a movie star."

She let her gaze roam over his crop of rumpled dark hair.

"He had black hair and blue eyes," she said, "and he told her he was Black Irish. Born and raised in Dublin, he had a thick brogue she found exciting. Being from a family where her grandparents had come over on the boat and who still spoke Irish Gaelic, she felt a kinship to Faulkner."

"A kinship he took advantage of," Julian said.

Kiley nodded. "She would go over to the carnie and talk with him, flirt with him, I imagine. One thing led to another and… Well, you get the picture."

"He got her pregnant."

"She had no way of knowing that until long after the carnie had moved on. She didn't even know his name. He'd told her to call him Irish. It wasn't until the show came back the next year that she saw him again, bringing their son along for him to see."

Julian snorted. "That must have pleased him."

"She also brought along her father, grandfather and three brothers," she said. "There had been a hasty marriage, performed by a priest in Des Moines who was willing to overlook the circumstances of the joining. The priest didn't inquire as to whether Jason Faulkner wished to do the right thing. From the two black eyes and the arm in a sling the carnie sported, the question hadn't been necessary.

"Fay's father brought her and her new family back to Riverside and bought them a used trailer to live in. There wasn't much money in the family but there was a lot of love. They didn't look down on Fay and apparently the town didn't, either. Faulkner was given a job—which he hated—and was more or less made to tow the line."

"Miserable the entire time, no doubt."

"He wasn't given much money but that didn't seem to hamper him. He slipped over to Iowa City quite a bit," Kiley told Julian. "Fay's father and brothers went after him and brought him back every time. Most times he was drunk and they found him with other women."

"How did he die?" Julian asked. He had a picture of his real father that wasn't all that much better than the adopted one he had grown to loathe.

"Life must have been hell for your mother. He beat her whenever he felt like it and took his anger out on you, too, it seems. The first year of your life, you were in and out of the ER with broken bones."

Julian rubbed his left arm. "I knew there were old breaks but I always thought Albert did it."

"He came home one night drunker than she had ever seen him, according to Fay. Apparently you were sitting in the middle of the floor, in his way, and he kicked you. He kicked you hard enough to put you in the hospital for nearly a week. They thought you were going to die."

Julian had a fleeting memory of being rocked, tears falling on his cheeks. He could hear the lullaby interspersed with sobs that shook the breast of the woman holding him.

"While you were still hospitalized, your grandfather went looking for Faulkner. He found him in the bedroom, lying face down on the floor. He'd been dead three days, shot between the eyes. Your mother was charged, pleaded temporary insanity and given twenty-five years to life. She served thirty years. From what Bennis learned, she was a model prisoner until one of the other inmates took a disliking to her and threatened to kill her. Your mother had never had any trouble before then but she knew women who had, true criminals, so she got a makeshift weapon from one of them to protect herself. Unfortunately, she had to use it against the woman who came after her. As a result, they tacked on more time to her sentence even though it was self-defense."

"That she served as long as she did is outrageous," Julian said through clenched teeth.

"In her file she states she got her G.E.D. as well as graduated college with a degree in accounting while she was in. She graduated with honors, at that."

"Must be where I get my math skills," he chuckled.

"So those years weren't entirely wasted even though she has never had to use her degree. Her husband never wanted her to work."

"Is she happy with Lynden?"

"According to her, she is. He is a well-respected city councilman from a rather wealthy Quad Cities family." At his inquiring look, she explained the meaning. "Davenport, Bettendorf, Moline, and Rock Island."

He shrugged, clearly not familiar with the geography in that part of the country.

"He was willing to spend as much money as needed to help her find you," she said quietly. "That should give you some indication of how he feels about her."

"He sounded protective," Julian said.

"I imagine he is," she said. "With good reason."

* * * * *

Later that morning when they had finished the flaky croissants and fresh fruit, Julian drank the last of the rich coffee in the silver pot and sat contemplating Kiley as she went about getting dressed for the day. He admired her shapely legs and silken hair, the way she moved, her mannerisms. He knew himself well enough to know he had fallen in love with this woman—and had fallen hard. When the phone rang, he motioned her away from it and took the call himself.

"She's not pleased, but then we knew she wouldn't be," Henri reported.

"Keep a watch on the situation," Julian suggested.

"Of course. She hasn't canceled the trip to Kingston and Bellington is scheduled to arrive in Miami late tomorrow morning."

"Let me know when he arrives. I think your suggestion is our best course of action."

"You want his ticket cancelled?" Henri asked after a moment of silence.

"Yes, I believe so. I don't think he needs to do any more traveling."

"I'll make sure he doesn't," Henri said then hung up.

"Who was that?" Kiley asked as she came into the living area of the suite. She was screwing a small gold hoop into her earlobe.

"Henri. We're having problems with one of the men," Julian said. "I've decided to retire him."

"Too old to pleasure the ladies, huh?" she laughed.

"'To everything there is a season'," he quoted.

She came over and sat in his lap, wrapping her arms around his neck. "What shall we do today?"

He wagged his brows at her. "I think I can come up with something," he said, lifting her in his arms and carrying her to the bed.

Chapter Fifteen

Celeste buckled her seatbelt tightly as the Lear began its decent to the Kingston airfield. Her expensive nails drummed an irritated rhythm on the padded arm cushion of her seat and her right foot waggled in a quick, round and round motion.

Pierce Umsted would have taken her hand but he was across the aisle. He knew there was nothing he could say to calm her, to tamp down the fury sparking in her black eyes. What she needed was a long, hard fuck that would leave her too breathless to think about Julian St. John.

"He's never denied me a visit to the Cay. Why now?"

Pierce shook his head. "I don't know, ma'am."

"Do you think that Trevor woman told him to cut his ties to me?"

Her words gave him an idea.

"That would be my guess, ma'am," he acknowledged.

Tears filled Celeste's eyes. "I'm losing him, Pierce. I'm losing the man I love."

It bothered Pierce that he couldn't get Celeste to love him as she loved Julian. He did almost everything she asked him to—outside something that would get him a lethal injection—but it seemed the more he did, the less inclined she was to see his real feelings for her. He had warmed her bed for ten years now and other than those times she journeyed to the Cay and the despicable arms of St. John, he warmed her body as well. As far as he knew, he and St. John were the only ones to know the treasures of Celeste's exquisite body and he wanted to keep it that way. Truth be told, the only man he felt he could murder and not regret it was Julian St. John. The more that hated name crossed his mind, the bleaker his situation seemed to be until it reached a red-hot point that prodded his male pride one time too many.

His anger, the unrelenting pain of hurt and rejection got the best of him and he blurted out, "Why do you want someone who doesn't want you? He doesn't love you. I doubt he feels anything for you except maybe gratitude. Why hold onto him?"

"I suggest," she said, her chin lifted, "you remember who it is that buys those designer shirts and slacks you love so well. I also suggest you remember that cocks are a dime a dozen in New Orleans and yours can be replaced at the drop of a hat."

Pierce narrowed his eyes. "And I suggest you remember that cunts get older quicker than cocks in New Orleans," he sneered.

Celeste blinked. *Now I hit a spot*, Pierce thought. No one had talked to her like that in decades—if ever. From the dagger glare she was shooting at him, he guessed that had she not been buckled in, she would have attacked him.

Then she surprised him. "Fuck me," she said.

"Fuck *me*," he returned, putting his hand to the zipper of his pants.

The plane was steeply angled, going in for its landing.

She watched him unbutton his fly, drag the zipper down and pull his cock out. He held it—fully erect. She moistened her lips.

"Or would you rather I just jerk off?" he inquired.

She unbuckled her seatbelt and managed to stagger her way to his seat. Holding his gaze with hers, she dropped to her knees.

"And make it good," he said.

Pierce's fingers dragged through her hair, positioning her above his throbbing cock. He laid his head back as she worked him like the expert she was. The suction of her lips on his flesh made his head pound as the blood rushed. The subservient position of her on her knees before him was a heady sensation he had not experienced since junior high school with the senior girl who could be had for the price of a reefer.

"Suck me," he ordered, his hips unconsciously lifting and lowering to her rhythm. "Take it all."

* * * * *

Clive Bellington detested public restrooms. He never felt them clean enough for his personal hygienic tastes. Neither did he like sharing a restroom—even one in the VIP lounge—with strangers. Habitually, after a long flight that included too much alcohol, his first stop upon arriving on American soil was to make a beeline to the facilities since they didn't let you get up once the plane started its descent.

"Check the room."

Hansen entered the restroom, was relieved to find it empty then came out to tell his employer he would have the facility to himself.

"Stand here and discourage anyone else from entering," Clive ordered Hansen.

Having had the same command thrown at him many times prior, Hansen merely nodded and took up a position in front of the door to the men's restroom. As planned, the VIP lounge was empty save for him and Bellington. When the door opened and three janitorial staff men walked in, Hansen relaxed and moved away from the door.

"Have a safe trip home," one of the janitors said quietly.

Hansen smiled and as he left the VIP lounge felt as though a huge weight had been lifted from his shoulders.

* * * * *

Fay Lynden put the receiver down and turned to her husband. "He wants us to fly to Kingston, Jamaica," she said. "He'll have a boat there to take us to him."

Brad took her into his arms. "How do you feel about that, Fay-Fay?"

Tears were streaming down Fay's face. "I'm going to see my Paddy," she said, her voice thick with emotion. "After all these years, I'm going to see my baby."

"He's not a baby anymore, darlin'," Brad reminded her. "A lot of water has passed under both your bridges."

"I know," she said, swiping a hand over her wet eyes. "But it doesn't matter. He knows why I went to prison and he said he understands."

"I'm sure he does, but you have to remember he's done a lot of things he's going to be ashamed for his mama to know. You're going to have to go easy on him."

"I'll have plenty of time to calm down," she said. "He can't send the boat for us for a few days. He has something he has to see to first."

"That's good 'cause I think you're gonna need those few days to rehearse what you want to say to him."

Fay shook her head. "I don't need time for that, Brad. I've had over thirty years to rehearse what I'll say."

* * * * *

Julian walked beside Henri along the beach. A storm was brewing off the coast and the waves were higher than normal. Overhead, the sky was dark gunmetal gray.

"It was such a lovely morning a few hours ago," Henri said with a sigh. "Now look at it."

"Any word from our man in Kingston?" Julian asked.

"Her plane landed about an hour ago. She's still onboard though the pilot and crew have disembarked." He cast Julian a jaded look. "Give you one guess what she's doing."

Julian rolled his shoulders. "I pity Umsted. She has a tendency to rake her nails down your back when she's angry and I imagine she's very unhappy with me right about now."

"She'll get over it," Henri snorted. "She's got lots of pretty boys to take her mind off you."

Julian stopped, picked up a piece of shell and sailed it out into the water. Hunkering down on the sand, he looked out across the sea. "Kiley called you a procurer and I said that wasn't what you did."

"I've been called worse," Henri admitted. He sunk to his haunches beside his friend.

"Why did you take me to Celeste, Henri?"

Henri gave a loud sigh. "I could see potential in your scrawny little ass," he said. "I would have taken you over to Warden's but you needed woman handling and not more of what you'd had too much of in England."

Julian felt a wave of anger grip him. "I'd have killed myself if you had taken me to Warden." He thought of the man who had eventually been found hanging in a field outside Metairie, his genitals gone. The man who had provided entertainment for New Orleans's wealthy pedophiles had not died an easy death.

Henri's mien turned serious. "You needed to disappear. People with money were looking for you and you needed the kind of protection the Quarter offered. It wasn't ideal, but it was the best this *procurer* could do for a half-dead twelve-year-old on the run."

"Why don't you just admit you trusted her to take care of me?" Julian asked.

Henri shrugged.

"You pretend as though you don't, but I know you like Celeste. You wouldn't have taken me there if you thought she would hurt me."

"I've taken in a lot of strays over the years, St. John," Henri said. "You were the only two-legged variety though." He shrugged again. "Call it a daddy complex. I saw a bit of me in you and wanted to protect you. I sure as hell couldn't take care of you, but I figured she would. I only wanted what was best for you and she echoed that feeling." He chuckled. "You were a pretty dismal-looking little rat when I took you to her. Now look at you."

"Thanks to you."

Henri grinned then waved his hand in front of his genitals. "It was Celeste that made a man of you. As I knew she would."

"Even though you would have preferred to do that yourself," Julian said quietly. He had always known which sex Henri enjoyed. He suspected Henri's affection for him went deeper than the strong friendship they shared.

Henri sniffed. "You have a very high opinion of yourself, don't you, St. John?" he asked. "Why would I want a skinny little twelve-year-old English muffin when I could have all the eighteen-year-old American biscuits I could grab?"

Julian laughed and stood up. He looked to Henri as he would have an older brother—a male who had protected him when he was a child. "English muffin, huh?"

"Oh, Lord, that accent. Tea and crumpets, don't you know?" Henri complained, standing up. "It set my nerves on edge. I'm glad you at least knew how to speak French."

Julian draped his arm over Henri's shoulders and they continued their walk, Henri's arm over Julian's.

"I'm glad you didn't want to butter this English muffin, Henri," Julian said.

"Never could stand those things," Henri complained. "Now a good French croissant or an American biscuit…"

* * * * *

Kiley listened with the receiver held away from her ear. Greg's anger was a tangible thing leaping out at her from all that distance. She had the feeling that had they been in the same room together, he would have slapped her. She had called to tell him to send her last paycheck, her part of the money for finding Fay Lynden's son. She had also called to tell him she wouldn't be coming back to Iowa and that even as she spoke to him, movers were packing her belongings up for shipment to Mistral Cay.

"What about Xander?" Greg bellowed. "Are you going to just leave that poor—"

She pulled the receiver to her ear. "You don't give a rat's ass about my cat, Greg," she snapped. "Don't you even think to try to guilt me about him. He's being taken care of, don't you worry."

"I guess you like that perverted lifestyle down there, huh?" Greg sneered. "Didn't get enough fucking yet?"

"Goodbye, Greg," Kiley said. "Screw only the ones who don't have a communicable disease."

With that she hung up. Her hands were trembling, her stomach sour and the blood was pounding in her ears. She disliked confrontations—even at a distance or on the impersonal Internet—and found them unsettling. Brooding about such things for hours, if not days, afterward was part of her personality.

"He didn't take it well, I gather," Julian remarked. "I imagine he hates losing you."

Kiley shrugged. "I think it's more of an ego thing with him. He likes things his way all the time."

Julian went to her and took her in his arms. He made no comment, only held her as she snuggled against him.

"What about Celeste?" she asked.

"What about her?"

"Do you think she'll keep trying to come to the Cay?"

"My men have orders not to allow her here," he replied. "She won't answer my phone calls, so screw her. I wanted to explain about you personally to her instead of having her take the word of her snitch, but if she doesn't want to talk to me about it, she'll just have to scratch her mad place."

"But if she was mad enough to send for your uncle, she is mad enough to try to cause you real problems."

"Let her," Julian said, his voice tight. "I'm not an altar boy, Kiley. I can fling shit with the best of them."

"Your uncle will—"

"That situation is being taken care of, sweetness," Julian told her. "I won't have to worry about him again."

A shudder passed through Kiley but she knew she would never ask what had occurred to rid her lover of his enemy.

* * * * *

"Did Mr. St. John receive my résumé?" Hansen asked Henri.

"Yes, indeed he has, mon ami. I am delighted to offer you employment here at the resort," Henri replied. "We recently lost our housekeeper. Would you be interested in that position?"

"Yes, indeed I would. I have no desire to go back to England."

"Completely understandable. I assume it will be a few days before you will be able to journey on to Kingston?"

"Yes, the police are investigating the shocking murder of my former employer. I will, of necessity, be obliged to remain here until matters are settled."

"Yes, of course," Henri agreed. "Please let us know if there is anything we can do to help speed up your arrival."

"Thank you, I will."

Henri hung up the phone and settled back in his plush leather chair. He had known James Hansen for a long time and had been paying the Dutchman to keep tabs on the Bellington household for over ten years.

He smiled. It had been nearly a decade since last he had shared his body with James and was looking forward to a renewal of their friendship.

Chapter Sixteen

Kiley watched her lover pacing the deck of *The Connemara* like the caged panther to which Dr. Carstairs had once likened him. His dark hair blew about his handsome face, tugging at his white silk shirt, but he seemed not to notice.

"Not black?" she had asked as he tucked the shirt into the waistband of a pair of gray slacks.

"This is my mother I am meeting," he answered, reaching up to remove the gold earring from his earlobe. "I want her to meet Patrick O'Reilly, not Julian St. John."

"Would you prefer I call you Patrick then?" she asked.

He had looked around at her. "Do you mind?" he inquired.

"No," she answered. "I haven't been sure whether to call you Sean or Julian or just plain old Sugar Buns." She grinned.

He rolled his eyes. "You'd better not," he warned then his lips twitched. "At least not around my mother."

As she watched him prowling the deck, she could not help but admire the sensuality of his movements. There was something primal—almost predatory—about the way he moved and she was reminded of the power and wealth this man wielded. One phone call had precipitated the removal of all her worldly goods from Iowa in the space of a few hours' time. The cost must have been astronomical but was most likely pocket change to a man like Julian. She corrected herself—like Patrick O'Reilly.

"They will begin building our home on the far side of the island next week," he had told her.

"Our home?"

"You don't think I would expect you to live at the resort, do you?" he queried.

"Even if I would prefer to do so?"

Her lover's eyes had narrowed dangerously. "Why? So you can look at naked men all day?" He shook his head. "I think not."

"So I could be near you?" she countered.

He thought about that then cocked one shoulder. "Flirt with even one helper, sweetness, and I'll have his balls on a tray to feed to my pet piranhas."

She blinked. "You have pet piranhas?"

"No flirting," was all he would say.

She now saw him walking toward her from the far end of the deck and smiled.

"I've been thinking," he said as he reached her. "I'm going to have them go through with building our house."

Kiley groaned. "Patrick, come on. I'm not going to—"

"I can't have my mother visiting me at the resort," he said. "I can't leave here and I would like to spend holidays with her." He leaned against the rail. "When I spoke with her this morning, she said there was no reason she couldn't come for Christmas and Thanksgiving, Easter, the Fourth of July."

"Yours and her birthdays," Kiley suggested quietly.

"Those, too," he agreed with an emphatic nod. "The yacht is acceptable but I'd like to have a porch to sit on, just looking out to sea, talking."

"If that's what you want, then that's what we'll have."

"And a nice place for you and me to say our vows," he added.

Kiley's mouth dropped open. "W-what?"

Before she could react, he lowered one knee to the deck and reached for her hand. "Silkeen Marie Trevor, would you do me the honor of becoming my wife?" he asked.

"Don't you ever call me Silkeen again," she insisted, her eyes flashing. "How did you find out—?"

"Kiley Marie Trevor," he interrupted, "would you do me the honor of becoming my wife?"

In the last twenty-four hours, she had come to realize she had fallen for this passionate man. She wanted nothing more than to spend her life with him. While she appeared to be thinking over the offer, he reached into his pocket and pulled out an engagement ring.

"It's only two carats," he explained as he paused with the ring just touching the nail of the third finger of her left hand. "If you want something larger, I—"

"No," she was quick to say. Ostentation had never appealed to her and diamonds larger than three carats had always seemed vulgar. Two carats was just right. "It's perfect."

He arched a thick dark brow.

"Yes," she said, tears glistening. "Oh, yes."

He slid the ring onto her finger then got to his feet, folding her into his arms and sealing their bargain with a kiss that made the toes in her sandals curl. She was only marginally aware of a strange sound above them as the man she loved pulled back from her.

Overhead, the sleek black helicopter from the Cay was flying parallel to *The Connemara* and the owner of Mistral Cay looked up. The chopper pilot gave his employer a thumbs-up then banked the expensive machine away from the ship.

"My mother should be here in a moment or two," Patrick O'Reilly said over the thump-thump-thump of the helicopter's blades. He turned so Kiley's back was to him, her body pressed closely to his.

Off to the starboard side of *The Connemara*, the yacht that had brought Kiley to the Cay sailed toward them.

She wrapped her arms over his, feeling the tremor shake his body.

They stood like that until the other yacht was riding at anchor beside them. A mile or so out to sea, the helicopter patrolled the air, making slow, lazy circuits. On the water, four runabouts carrying armed men secured the waves. Onboard *The Connemara*, the crew was armed to the teeth.

"I'll not take any chances with you or my mother," Patrick had pronounced.

That he feared trouble from Celeste was evident in the way his eyes kept scanning the horizon.

"There she is," he whispered.

An older woman was being helped into the yacht's lifeboat. Beside her, a man looked across at them and waved. Turning to the woman as he joined her in the lifeboat, he pointed to where Patrick and Kiley stood.

"She's beautiful," Kiley said softly.

"Yes," Patrick agreed.

It seemed an eternity before Fay Lynden and her husband Bradford were brought onboard *The Connemara*. When at last she stepped onto the deck of her son's yacht, she seemed unable to go any further. She stood there with her husband's arm wrapped securely around her shoulder.

Realizing the man she loved did not seem able to move either, Kiley eased his arms from her and walked to the Lyndens. She put out a hand. "I'm Kiley Trevor, Mrs. Lynden."

Fay took the young woman's hand then pulled her into a very strong embrace. "Thank you," she said forcefully. "Thank you so much for finding my son."

"Yes," Bradford said, patting Kiley's arm. "We appreciate all you've done."

Fay released Kiley but still seemed unsure of herself. She was facing her son, both of them smiling at the other, even though neither seemed able to traverse the distance between them.

"What would you say to a nice tall Tom Collins, Mr. Lynden?" Kiley asked, threading her arm through his.

"I'd say lead the way," Bradford chuckled.

Kiley kept up a quiet conversation with Bradford, introducing him to Henri as they made their way into the interior of the yacht.

* * * * *

Alone on the deck, mother and son took a hesitant step toward another, stopped almost in unison then laughed together at their nervousness.

Fay opened her arms.

Her son hurried to her.

He enveloped her in a hug that could have crushed her had she been of less stalwart stock. Her tears mingling with his as she brought his face to hers to kiss him lightly on the lips, she heard his low whimper of hurt.

"It's all right now, Paddy," she said, bringing his head to her shoulder though he towered over her. "Mama's here, baby."

His body was shaking with the force of his sobs. He wanted to drop to his knees and hold onto her, press his cheek to her belly, lower his head to her lap. He wanted to feel the gentle stroke of her hand on his hair and hear her crooning to him as the faceless woman of his memories had for as long as he could remember.

* * * * *

"I thought she'd wear a hole in the floor of the ship," Bradford said after taking a long sip of his frosty Tom Collins.

"Him, too," Kiley laughed.

"He was as nervous as a long-tail cat in a room full of rocking chairs," Henri put in.

"Everything's gonna be okay now," Bradford predicted with a sigh.

"Let's hope so," Henri said, casting Kiley a quick look.

"She's not in the best of health," Bradford told them, "but I think seeing him is the best medicine she could get."

As the two men talked, Kiley left the bar and with drink in hand walked to the open doorway. She saw Fay leading her son to a brace of deck chairs. They sat down on the chairs, facing one another, holding hands.

It seemed too intimate a moment upon which to be spying but Kiley felt protective of this man—even though she was relieved things were going as she had hoped.

* * * * *

"Were they good to you?" Fay asked and her hand tightened on her son's.

"I had the best of everything," Patrick answered. "The best clothes, the best school. I never lacked for anything money could buy."

Vividly aware her son had not answered her question, Fay looked out across the waves. The conversation she'd had the day before with Greg Strickland was still fresh in her mind.

"He's wanted in Louisiana for murder and the police are pretty sure he hired a man to kill his uncle, Sir Clive Bellington," Greg had told her. "So far, they haven't been able to prove it but there's a detective on the case who won't stop until St. John is brought to justice."

"Do you love her?" Fay asked, returning her gaze to her son.

"With all my heart," Patrick answered.

"Does she love you?"

"Yes, ma'am. She's agreed to marry me," he said with pride shining in his tearful eyes.

"How wonderful. Congratulations. Then I see no reason why you would need to ever leave your island," she said.

Patrick swiped at a tear. "Mama, I can't leave. I—"

"He was a son of a bitch," Fay said, breaking off his words. "I thought I loved him but he'd beat me in places where the bruises wouldn't show. If your grandfather and uncles had ever seen me bruised, I think they would have saved me the trouble of putting a slug between his eyes." She held her son's stare. "I have no doubt he'd have wound up killing me one day. Some men just plain deserve killing." She squeezed his hands. "Don't you think so, Paddy?"

He understood what she meant and nodded. "You know about my past," he said.

"I know it doesn't matter. Sometimes we do what we have to in order to survive, Paddy. Sometimes we do it to protect others and sometimes to protect ourselves."

"Even if we've done things that are unforgivable?"

"You are my son, my child. If you have done things that were necessary to keep yourself safe, there is nothing to forgive." She took his hand and brought it to her cheek, turning her face to kiss his palm. "I never stopped looking for you and not once have I ever stopped loving you, Paddy."

Her gentle words and loving eyes were his undoing. He broke down again, sobbing like a child. His shoulders shaking, he bent over in his pain, his arms wrapped around his chest.

Fay slipped to her knees beside him and drew his head to her shoulder. She encircled him in a tight embrace then began humming the Connemara Cradle Song, rocking him in her arms as he released the years of hurt and sorrow that had been his life.

Chapter Seventeen

Kiley wiped at a tear and turned away. Henri was standing a few feet behind her.

"May I have a word with you in private, Miss Trevor?" he asked in his thick French accent.

"Of course, Mr. Bouvier, but please call me Kiley," she replied.

Henri nodded. "Only if you call me Henri," he responded.

They walked to the stateroom that was Henri's own quarters aboard *The Connemara*. After asking his guest to be seated, he closed and locked the door.

"This is one of the few places onboard that has not been bugged," Henri explained. "We can talk freely here."

Kiley arched a graceful brow. "Is there something you don't want Patrick to know about?"

Henri waved a hand. "Patrick. Anthony. Julian. Sean…" He sighed. "I know he wants to be called Patrick from now on but Julian is the man I know and Julian is how I will always think of him."

"You and he are very close, aren't you?"

A wide smile stretched Henri's rugged face. "Did he tell you I saved his life?"

"Not once but twice," she answered.

"And that I am the best administrative assistant he has ever had?"

"I believe he said you were the only administrative assistant he has ever had," Kiley laughed.

"Did he tell you that I am madly, deeply in love with him?" Henri asked in a droll voice.

"No, I don't believe he did."

"Well, I am," Henri said and his smile slipped slowly away. He held Kiley's gaze and when she didn't so much as bat an eye at his admission, he relaxed. "I really am, you know," he finished quietly.

Kiley merely smiled. She knew there was nothing she could say that would be of any help to the man seated in the chair opposite her.

"I am happy for him that he has found you," Henri said. He crossed his right ankle over his left knee and tugged at the pant cuff. "He deserves good things in this life."

"After such a terrible childhood?" Kiley asked, letting Henri know—if he didn't already—that Patrick had confided in her.

"When I opened that crate," Henri said, "as soon as he opened his eyes I knew." He sighed. "I knew because I recognized the signs of abuse in that helpless, hopeless gaze."

"Yet you took him to a woman who conceivably could have abused him in a different way," Kiley accused before she could stop herself. When she started to apologize, Henri held his hand up.

"Celeste was raped when she was nine years old," he confided to Kiley. "She too knew what had happened to this poor, starving child. She sent me for the physician who saw to her workers and while I was fetching him, she bathed Ju—" He shook his head. "He was Anthony back then. She sat up all night with him, holding him in her arms, crooning to him. I was across the room on a pallet should I be needed and the doctor was in the next room. We took turns feeding that little boy small amounts of water and broth, wiping away the sweat from a fever we were sure would claim him before the night was through. By morning, he was sleeping deeply but he was a long way from being out of danger."

"How old were you?" Kiley asked.

Henri's brow furrowed. "Nineteen, I believe. I had been in America four years." He shrugged. "I, too, had been a stowaway when the ship's cook found me." He looked away. "I more than paid for my passage to America on that devil ship, believe me."

"You had been molested, too," she said quietly. "On the ship?"

"Oh, long before that, *petite*." Henri shrugged. "Over and over before I was barely old enough to smell my own pee, as the saying goes." He grinned. "To you Midwesterners that's the Southern way of saying puberty."

Kiley smiled at him. "I figured as much." She cocked her head to one side in sympathy. "Who abused you, Henri?"

"Who didn't?" he asked, laughing. "My father, his cronies, several boys at school." He threw out a hand. "I was a skinny kid, unable to protect myself. I was ripe for the picking, as they say. It didn't help I had a face like a choirboy."

"Well, at least you weren't molested by a member of the clergy," she said, picking up on the choirboy comment, but at Henri's raised eyebrow, she put a hand to her mouth. "Really?"

"Good old Father Jacques. May he be roasting o'er a slow pit in the hottest part of hell." He drew in a long breath then released it. "I jumped from the frying pan directly into the fire when I hid on that ship but I didn't know—have any idea about the flames of hell until I hopped a freight train in South Carolina." He looked off in the distance. "There were a couple of hobos who nearly killed me that night then tossed me off the train into a ditch." He shrugged again. "I would have died if Padilla hadn't come along."

"Padilla?" Kiley questioned.

"He was connected, as they say," Henri explained. "Imagine my surprise when this big, burly Italian man picks me up outta the ditch and takes me home with him. Took good care of me. Never once laid a hand to me that wasn't a gentle touch. He became the father I never really had. I became the son he'd lost to the Vietnam War. Despite what he was—and believe me, a boy of fifteen being cosseted by an honest-to-goodness American wiseguy was absolute heaven to me—I was in awe of him. He introduced me to people in his line of work—contacts that have come in handy on occasion— and he taught me things I never would have learned otherwise."

"Such as?"

"How to track a man," Henri said, turning to look here in the eye. "How to kill an enemy with the least noise. The correct way to hold a blade, a garrote, a nine millimeter, a Molotov cocktail, and make the best use of each one."

"You've killed a man, too," Kiley said, shivering despite the calm look on Henri's face.

"Men," he corrected. "I've killed several men. Every one deserved it. Most were pedophiles and one bled to death in the bayou after losing a couple of portions of his anatomy."

Kiley ran her hands up and down her arms. "Did you do any of that protecting Patrick?"

"Some of it," he answered. "There isn't anything I wouldn't do for him. I'd give my life if he asked me to. He's the only person I've ever loved."

"Yet you took him to a known madam," she accused. "Why her?"

"I did security work for her," Henri stated. "That and a little petty larceny on the side wasn't a bad living for a nineteen-year-old

French transplant." He chuckled. "She didn't have to worry about me sampling her girls. I wasn't interested."

"But she had boys, too," Kiley said.

Once more that fatalistic Gallic shrug shifted his brawny shoulders. "Well, those she didn't worry about if they were for male trade. I just couldn't touch those earmarked for the female trade." He sighed. "Like a certain handsome ex-English muffin we know."

"You've been together ever since the day you found him."

"That we have. He was a scrawny, shy and terribly down-beaten twelve-year-old."

"Why didn't you stay with Padilla?" she asked, curious.

That shrug showed itself again. "We had a falling out over a certain matter best left unmentioned," Henri said. "It was a private matter between him and me."

"Oh," Kiley said.

"You're more curious about the muffin than me, though, aren't you?" he teased.

She nodded, blushing.

"So what else do you want to know?"

"How old was he when she took his virginity?" Kiley wanted to know.

Henri's grin was almost sinister. "Old enough to want what she was offering," he answered.

"Did he have a choice?"

Henri held his hands out in the typical French fashion. "One does what one must," he replied. "Yes, he felt obligated to her for helping to save his life, for the clothes on his back and the food in his belly. He also knew she would not make him pleasure other women if he didn't want to."

"And how old was he when he decided he wanted to share his expertise with other women?" she mumbled.

"I believe he was seventeen," Henri told her.

"She'd been teaching him since he was how old?"

The Frenchman clucked his tongue. "Fourteen, fifteen. I don't remember."

"Oh, my God," Kiley groaned. "That is disgusting."

"What is disgusting about being taught the correct way to make love?" Henri inquired. "How to please your partner as well as yourself? How to keep from getting a girl pregnant?" He leered sternly at his guest. "She taught him many important life lessons, Kiley, not just the art of seduction."

"I'm surprised she shared him at all," Kiley said.

"Ah, but there is possession and there is obsession," Henri stated, the index finger of his right hand held aloft. "She thought she possessed him mind, body and soul, and when she discovered she did not, that he wanted someone closer to his own age... I believe she was twenty-five when she took him the first time. By the time his eye began roaming, she was in her thirties and beginning to feel the fear that comes with that age."

"He found someone in whom he was interested," Kiley said, "and Celeste felt threatened."

"Threatened is not the word to describe how she reacted," Henri said. "She was terrified he would leave her. The possession had turned to obsession. She would have done anything to keep him with her."

Kiley frowned. "What did she do?"

Henri uncrossed his legs and stood up. He walked to his well-stocked bar and turned to ask if she wanted something.

"Maybe later," Kiley said, sensing something bad was about to be revealed.

When he had poured himself a healthy measure of cognac, he returned to his chair, sat down and took a sip of the potent brew before taking a deep breath, releasing in and continuing his tale.

"He turned twenty-one on November third," he remembered. "We all gave him little presents because not a one of us did not like the young man Celeste had named Julian St. John." He grinned. "Julian after a character in an American film about a gigolo and St. John after an actress she believed she resembled."

"What did you give him?"

"A bottle of his favorite cologne," Henri replied, "which, believe me, was not cheap."

"What did Celeste give him?"

"A Mercedes convertible," Henri said. "Black with tan leather upholstery." He took a sip of the cognac. "But it was what Franchine gave him that caused all the trouble."

"Franchine?"

"One of Celeste's girls," Henri explained. "A beautiful octoroon from Metairie. Ah, she was breathtaking. A bit shy but an expert in the ways of love." He shook his head. "Had my affections not leaned in a different direction, I might well have sampled that lovely's wares, believe me."

"I take it she and Julian became lovers," Kiley said, a bit of jealousy making her squirm in her chair.

"That was her gift to him," Henri agreed. "Before that, she was only sent to important businessmen, older men who—though they were kind and generous to her—were never handsome and virile as was Julian."

"So she was as eager for a young lover as he was," Kiley suggested for clarification.

"I think so."

"What happened when Celeste found out?"

"All hell broke loose," Henri answered with a grimace. He finished off his cognac and sat with the glass balanced on his knee. "She found them together and I thought she would tear Franchine apart with her bare hands. As it was, she had one of her bodyguards drag the naked girl out of Julian's bed and out of his life forever."

"She had the girl killed?" Kiley gasped.

Henri shook his head. "That would have been far better than the revenge Celeste exacted on that poor girl." He held Kiley's gaze. "She sold her to a pig of an Arab who was always snooping around for girls to take back to the Middle East. No reputable madam or pimp would do business with the filthy bugger, but for this once, Celeste made an exception."

"Did she let Patrick's uncle know where he was?"

"She wouldn't have taken such a chance with his life. I honestly don't know how Bellington found out. I wish I did and I'm sure Celeste would have liked to have known who did it."

"You saved Patrick's life back then," Kiley said.

"He would have died had I not gotten him to Celeste's physician. As it was, he lost a kidney."

"And wound up here."

"It is paradise, is it not?" Henri asked. He waved his hand before him. "Warm, tropical breezes, turquoise water, lush beaches. What better place to have a nudist colony? One catering to the rich and bored?"

"You've helped him run it."

"I do whatever my friend does not want to do or dirty his hands in. I look after him and always will. It is his best interests that concern me, Miss Trevor. I will always be there for him should he have need of me."

"And having him here didn't bother Celeste? Being apart from him like this?"

"Oh, it bothered her," Henri said. "And she was still furious over what Bellington had done. Had that bastard not run like the coward he was, she would have sent someone to cut his throat. He was on a plane back to England with a contingent of bodyguards surrounding him at all times before she had a chance to have him killed."

"He went back to England only after he gave his statement to the police, though. Right?" Kiley asked.

Henri shifted in his chair. "Not exactly."

Kiley stared at her companion for a long time, neither of them speaking. When she finally broke the silence, her heart was trip hammering in her chest.

"Did the man he stabbed die?"

Henri looked up. "Oh, he died, but it wasn't at Julian's hands," he told her.

"You?"

Henri shrugged. "Do you think either Celeste or I would have let the bastard live after nearly killing the man we loved?"

Kiley drew in a long, shaky breath then her shoulders slumped as she exhaled. "It's not that he can't go back to the States, it's that you can't, so you won't allow him to."

"He has always been safer here," Henri defended his actions. "Here, he is his own master and—"

"But he's also a prisoner," Kiley stated.

"A much-loved and well-cared-for prisoner," Henri said with a twist of his lips.

Kiley folded her arms over her chest. "You need to tell him, Henri."

Shock widened the eyes of the Frenchman. "Oh, but I could never do that," he gasped. "He must never know."

"Then why tell me if you don't want him to find out?"

Anger briefly tightened the rugged face of Henri Bouvier. He ran his hand through his perfect haircut, mussing the thick salt-and-pepper hair. "He loves you," he said as though that would explain everything.

"He loves you, too," Kiley said softly.

"Yes, but not in the way I would like him to," Henri grated.

"Perhaps not, and though I understand why you have kept him in the dark all these years, you know in your heart he should be told the truth. He needs to know he isn't responsible for that man's death."

Henri got up and began pacing. He stopped at the porthole and looked out across the waves. "If he goes back to the States, I would lose him."

"We'll take it one step at a time," Kiley said, standing. "If you don't want to tell him he's not the killer he thinks he is, I'll do it. Either way, he should be able to tell his mother that he can come to visit her in the States."

Chapter Eighteen

Pierce Umsted was in a good place for once in his life. As he lay in the bed aboard the rented yacht, things could not have been more to his liking. Celeste had agreed to go back to New Orleans and not try to see St. John. She was cutting her ties to the bastard and that suited Pierce's plans. With her former lover out of the picture, Pierce could move into a position of power that had once belonged to Julian. He glanced at the door to their stateroom's bathroom where she was taking her morning soak and smiled. When she kicked the bucket, the brothel would become his and his alone.

A discreet knock on the cabin door sent Pierce to the portal. He opened it to find the steward standing there with an armful of linens.

"We didn't ask to have the bed changed," Pierce complained.

"Too bad," the steward said. "A change has been ordered."

As the linens fell away to reveal a semi-automatic pistol pointed directly at his chest, Pierce took one step back. He never took another before the hollow-point bullets ripped into his flesh, through his body and plowed into the wall behind him.

*****

The sky overhead was turning a darker gray as the steward walked down the steps of the Lear and climbed into the waiting sedan that had brought him to the jet.

"In for more rain, eh, old man?" the driver inquired as he put the car in gear.

"Looks a bit like home, don't you think?" the steward countered. He pulled out his cell phone, punched in a number then put the expensive little gadget to his ear. When the call was answered, he told the party on the other end that the job had been done.

"I am so pleased," Edwina Bellington said. "Do hurry home, Reginald. I hear a hurricane is headed for that part of the world."

*****

When she rang off, Edwina sat down at her writing desk and signed the solicitor's papers that would give her entire portion of the Bellington estate to her adopted son Anthony. For the last two days, she had listened to the solicitor give her a breakdown of Clive's estate and what was left of Albert's. She was stunned to learn the amount registered in the billions. Along with that bit of information had come another.

"Sir Clive kept a safety deposit box with information he believed you had the right to see should he precede you in death," the solicitor had explained. He'd handed Edwina a key. "I believe there might be papers you would not wish the tabloids to get into their smarmy hands."

An hour after the solicitor left, Edwina bade her driver bring the car around. Before the afternoon was over, she had learned things that had staggered her to the core of her being. Not only had Clive kept a thorough journal of every sordid, repulsive conquest—either willing or forced—that he and Albert had enjoyed over their lifetimes, as well as a meticulous diary with day-to-day happenings narrated in vivid detail, he had an address book with a comprehensive list of people and places with which he had contact.

Among that list was the new name and location of the adopted son she had begrudgingly come to love over the twelve years she had been his mother.

Anger replaced the shock of her discovery then mortal shame that she had been either unwilling or unable to see the abuse the boy had endured while in her care. Finding out the man she loved had methodically violated Anthony, had ordered him killed, and had nearly succeeded in his brutal quest, had brought Edwina to the brink of madness. In her misery, she had taken the souvenir Clive had brought back from a holiday jaunt to Germany and had placed it on her desk beside her writing pad, turning to look at it often as she wrote a note to Anthony, begging his forgiveness for her years of neglect.

With Clive gone—his memory now a revolting one that brought hot bile to her throat—and her unwilling complicity in the torment of a child who wanted nothing more than to be her son, Edwina had no desire to continue. She picked up that shiny little souvenir from Germany—that pretty little Beretta—placed it to her temple and pulled the trigger.

Chapter Nineteen

It had been a long day and Kiley was bone tired as she trudged up the stairs to her bedroom, pulling the tails of her silk blouse from her skirt as she went. She had left her high heels in the mudroom, reveling in the feel of the polished oak floor beneath the soles of her feet, and the sculptured pile of the carpet runner on the stairs soothed her bare toes as she climbed. Unbuttoning the garment as she walked down the hallway, she yawned widely, her body feeling the strain of a day meeting and greeting the Cay's clients. Pausing at the bedroom door, she flicked open the cuffs of the blouse and entered the darkened room. Reaching to her left, she fumbled for the light switch.

Without warning, a strong, powerful arm enclosed her waist in a firm grip that pressed the air from her lungs. A hand went over her mouth and she was lifted from the floor, her bare feet kicking out at her abductor.

"Be still or I'll make you regret it," her attacker hissed in her ear.

Kiley went still as she was carried toward the bed. Sucking in air through her nose, she grunted as she was tossed to the mattress and a heavy body fell atop her, pinning her to the silky coverlet.

"Do what I tell you and everything will work out just fine," the man lying on her said. "You understand?"

Attempting to nod beneath the unyielding hand plastered over her mouth, Kiley felt herself being turned over to her back. Unable to see the man now straddling her hips in the lightless room, she knew better than to struggle.

"I'm going to take my hand off your mouth," he told her. "I don't think I have to tell you what will happen if you scream."

Quivering, her heart pounding in her chest, she lay still as she felt him shift his weight, dragging something out from beneath the pillow. Eyes wide, Kiley felt her wrists looped together with a restraint she realized must be the belt to her terrycloth robe. Her attacker dragged her arms up by the bonds then tied them to the brass headboard above her. Before she could do more than whimper, a silken scarf was thrust between her lips and tied behind her head.

"I'm not taking any chances with you," he spat.

Helpless, at her attacker's mercy, Kiley closed her eyes as he slid down in the bed, pushing her legs wide with his knees and made quick work of tying her ankles to the footboard. The only sound she made was when the cold metal touched her knee and she heard the click of scissors as he began cutting away the expensive wool material from her body. She grunted with anger, her eyes flying up at the indignity of having one of her favorite skirts ruined.

"Like you don't have the money to buy a new skirt," he taunted, running the sharp blade up the fabric to expose her half-slip.

Within the space of five minutes or less, her attacker had bared her trembling body to his view and wadded her demolished clothing in a ball, tossing it into the wastebasket beside the bed. Naked, a cool draft playing over her goose bump-speckled flesh, she groaned as he left the bed and she heard the snick of the bedroom door lock engaging.

"Don't want to be interrupted now, do we?" he chuckled as he flipped on the light.

Kiley blinked against the intrusion of the harsh light from the dual lamps perched atop the bedside tables. For the first time, she got a good look at her attacker and a breath caught in her throat.

He was dressed entirely in black—silk long-sleeve shirt, leather breeches with a broad silver buckle at his waist. On his feet were black boots adorned with a silver design at the toe. Halfway down his face, a mask covered his forehead and nose, cheekbones and the color of his hair. Only his eyes showed behind the black fabric and those pale amber orbs glowed with purpose.

"I've been watching you," he said, his large hands going to the buttons of his shirt. "I've been waiting for a moment like this. I've wanted you beneath me from the first time I saw you."

Kiley flinched as he tore at the silk shirt, popping the buttons as he ripped the garment open. Her eyes flared at the sight of a broad chest covered with thick dark curls. As he shrugged out of the shirt, she felt a tremor pass through her lower belly for he was well built with washboard abs and chiseled pecs that made her mouth go dry. As his hands went to the wide leather belt at his slim waist, she looked away.

"Don't like what you see?" he asked, his tone tight. "Well, that's just too damned bad. You're going to get it whether you like it or not."

Struggling now against the bonds that held her to the bed, Kiley refused to look at her attacker. She felt the mattress sag as he sat down beside her. She heard him grunt then winced as first one heavy boot then the other hit the uncarpeted floor. When he stood up, she tensed, listening as he made quick work of divesting himself of the leather britches. When the mattress sagged once more she groaned; the heat of his nude body pressed intimately against her left side as he stretched out beside her.

"I want you to look at me," he said, reaching out to splay his hand around the column of her throat. Gently he caressed her slender neck then cupped her chin to turn her face toward him, his thumb stroking the line of her jaw.

Kiley stared into his masked face, her gaze riveted to the merciless depths of his eyes. He was looking back at her with a slight smile on his full lips. As she trembled, the smile became a knowing grin, the gleam of his white teeth contrasting sharply with the deep tan of his skin.

"I won't hurt you if you don't give me any guff," he promised. "Hell, you might even like what I'm going to do to you, baby."

A wild grunt of denial pushed from Kiley's throat and she stopped breathing as the grin disappeared from his face.

"You don't think so?" he growled. "Well, we'll see about that."

He moved his hand to the center of her chest, his fingers spread so the tips of his thumb and little finger grazed her nipples, linking both her breasts with an electrical surge of sensation that rippled like summer lightning through her body.

Kiley groaned, hating the treacherous stirrings that were building within her. She felt a chill go down her spine for she had seen the knowing look that had made his amber orbs sparkle.

"You like that, do you?" he challenged. He slid his hand over her right breast and cupped it.

Screaming her denial beneath the gag, Kiley pulled at her restraints, striving to arch her body from contact with his. His low chuckle of amusement narrowed her eyes as she turned her head to glare at him.

"It doesn't matter whether you like it or not," he said with a long sigh. "I'm going to enjoy it." His tone changed, the words becoming harsh as he said, "Let's you and me have some fun."

He turned his hand over and ran the backs of his fingers down the slope of Kiley's breast. Arcing his fingertips beneath the weight of her silken orb, he could feel the wild beat of her heart vibrating against the callused pads.

"I can play you," he whispered, lowering his lips to her ear, "like a finely tuned guitar."

Kiley whimpered behind the gag wedged between her trembling lips. She closed her eyes, willing her treacherous body not to respond to the warmth of his breath and pulled against the rough terrycloth that bound her wrists.

"You pretend you don't like it," he said as he eased his hand over her breast, nestling in his hot palm, "but you do. You revel in it, don't you, little cat?"

Heavy moistness throbbed between Kiley's spread legs and she jerked her bound ankles inward in a vain attempt to hide her vulnerability. Sweat dotted her upper lip, ran down her heaving sides. The heat from his nude body pressed down the full length of her left side and the musky smell of his cologne, the powerful male scent of him, made her face feel as though she faced a roaring fire.

"Should I touch you where you crave it most?" he purred, squeezing her breast gently. Her groan of pleasure-shame brought a low laugh from his throat. "I take that as a yes," he chuckled.

Panting beneath the constriction of the gag, Kiley inhaled suddenly through her nose as his fingernails grazed the areola of her breast before plucking at the nipple. Capturing the turgid bud between his thumb and forefinger, he began working it gently back and forth. She could not stop the grunt of pleasure that rippled through her.

His tongue spiraled around the outer rim of her ear then flicked swiftly into the sensitive center, eliciting a responsive tremor that rippled violently through Kiley's body.

"My little whore," he breathed. "My sweet, helpless little whore."

Once more the searing warmth of his palm flattened against her breast then began moving downward over the sweaty plane of her chest. Past the smooth indention of her quivering belly, over the sleek coarseness of her pubic hair, that demanding instrument of single-minded torture slipped unerringly between her legs to cup her very essence.

A groan of need echoed in Kiley's throat. Her hips arched upward from the mattress as she pressed her core against the invasion of his hand. Eyes flaring wide, nostrils drawing in labored breaths, she could feel the pulsation of his blood traveling along his long fingers, transmitting that pounding rhythm to her receptive lips, dragging from her a response she could not contain. Wetness oozed forth, seeping like dew falling from a rose at dawn.

"You are mine, little cat," he whispered. "Never forget that."

His middle finger drew upward, lightly traveling the valley between her nether lips, and then slid authoritatively into her moist center, driving deep.

Kiley thought she would pass out from the sheer intensity of the sensation focused between her open legs. The heat of his palm cupped possessively around her, the conquering invasion of his finger, made it impossible for her to do more than produce a muffled growl, the susurration nothing more than a keening sound of submission.

He withdrew his finger slightly and at her whimper of denial, he smiled, gazing into her pleading eyes with a knowing look. The finger returned to its pebbled depths, probing as deeply as its length would allow.

Sighing with relief, Kiley closed her eyes, squeezing them tightly as his finger began moving in a small circle within her silken depths.

"There was a time when I would have allowed you to lie there so passively, my precious whore," he said. Lifting his leg, he ran the sole of his foot along her shin from ankle to knee and back again. "I would have taken you quickly as you deserve then left you to that impotent fool you call your husband."

Kiley's eyes flew open and she glared at her tormentor. She pulled angrily against the bonds, grunting beneath the restriction of the gag.

He laughed at her fury. "Ah, you do hate me to insult that worthless sap, don't you?" Her growl seemed to amuse him more and a sparkle entered his amber eyes for a moment before his smile fled, his jaw clenched. With a look that sent a shudder of apprehension through his victim, he thrust two more fingers inside her, stretching the tender flesh.

"Bitch," he hissed, twisting his fingers, withdrawing them then driving again deeply. "I'll make you forget him or die trying."

Whimpering with barely restrained passion, Kiley levered her hips upward, striving to impale her lower body on the power of his questing hand.

"I want you to feel me, little cat," he vowed. "I want you to—"

The jarring intrusion of the telephone made Kiley groan with frustration. She watched her attacker jerk the receiver up and bark at the caller. So close was the attacker's face to hers, she could hear the conversation from the other end.

"I hate to bother you, but—"

"Then don't."

"I thought you might like to know your mother is in the lobby," Henri whispered.

"What?" Patrick shouted, sitting up. His eyes were wide, his face beet red.

"She just hiked across the island and she and Bradford are talking to Derek about getting circum—"

"I'll be right there."

Kiley sighed. "No more playtime, huh?"

Patrick glanced down at her. "I'll make it up to you tonight." He reached out to stroke her face. "What do you desire this evening, milady?"

Kiley thought about it for a moment. "We haven't done the savage Indian and captive white woman yet, have we?"

Her husband grinned. "No."

She yawned. "Go see what Fay wants then get back here, Sugar Buns, while I'm still in the mood for love."

He was out of the bed like a shot, ducking into the bathroom of their new Victorian-era-styled house. She lifted her head and through the open door watched him jabbing his arms into a white cotton shirt then stabbing the shirttail into a pair of faded blue jeans. He disappeared for a moment and the smell of that expensive French men's cologne Henri gave him twice yearly—birthday and at Christmas—wafted back to her. She smiled at him when he reappeared, hopping on one foot as he jammed his other foot into a sneaker.

"Calm down," she recommended.

"She is at the resort," he complained. "At the *resort*! I'm going to have a long talk with my mother."

She turned her head as he stomped to the door, his shoulders hunched as though the weight of the world had suddenly settled upon them.

"Paddy?" she called out in a sweet voice.

"Um," he replied as he jerked open the bedroom door.

"Do you think you could untie me before you go?"

TRADEMARK ACKNOWLEDGMENTS

The author acknowledges the trademarked status and trademark owners of the following wordmarks mentioned in this work of fiction:

Taco Tuesday: Gregory Hotel, Inc. aka The New Gregory's Corporation

Oscar: Academy of Motion Picture Arts and Science Corporation

Mr. Universe: World Physique Federation

Rolex: Rolex Watch U.S.A., Inc.

Colt Peacemaker: Colt's Manufacturing Company Corporation

Stetson: John B. Stetson Company

Lone Ranger: Golden Books Publishing Company, Inc.

Porsche: Dr. Ing. h.c. F. Porsche Aktiengesellschaft Corporation

Lear: Learjet Inc.

Mont Blanc: Montblanc-Simplo GmbH Corporation

Mercedes: Daimler Chrysler AG Corporation

Beretta: Fabbrica D'Armi P. Beretta, S.P.A. Corporation

ABOUT THE AUTHOR

Charlee, as she is known to her readers, is the author of 100 novels, the first ten of which are the WindLegend Saga. She was married 43 years to her high school sweetheart, Tom, until his untimely death in April 2009. She is the mother of two grown sons, Pete and Mike, and the proud grandmother of Preston Alexander and Victoria Ashley and the giddy great-grandmother of Amber Dawn.

A native of Sarasota, Florida, Charlee was adopted at birth and grew up in Colquitt and Albany, Georgia. She says of her heritage: "I was born in Florida and raised in Georgia, so that makes me an official Sunshine Cracker!" She now lives in the Midwest where she enjoys the changing of the seasons.

Her hobbies are reading, writing, and quietly communing with her beloved husband, Buddha Belly, as he guides her gently from somewhere beyond the here and now. She is owned and operated by seven cats who only allow her to leave the house for catnip, kitty kibble, and clumping kitty litter.

She loves to watch *ANYTHING* in which **Allan Hawco**, Michael Trucco, Victor Webster, or Chris Vance have starred, and patterns her heroes after these fine actors as her tribute to the many hours of enjoyment they have given her.

She collects statues of the Grim Reaper, Anubis, gargoyles, and windchimes. One of her prized possessions is a Grim Reaper windchime sent to her by a fan from England.

Her signature Reaper novels have a huge loyal following and currently she is at work on a new dark fantasy set in Australia.

Did you enjoy this book? Drop us a line and say so! We love to hear from readers, and so do our authors. To connect, visit www.boroughspublishinggroup.com online, send comments directly to info@boroughspublishinggroup.com, or friend us on Facebook and Twitter. And be sure to check back regularly for contests and new releases in your favorite subgenres of romance!

Are you an aspiring writer? Check out www.boroughspublishinggroup.com/submit and see if we can help you make your dreams come true.